CLEAT

Celia Aaron
Sloane Howell

WILL HE LOSE
THE PERFECT CATCH?

*SLOANE
HOWELL*

*Thanks for
reading!
xoxo,
Celia
Aaron*

CLEAT CATCHER

Celia Aaron & Sloane Howell

Copyright © 2016 Celia Aaron & Sloane Howell

"I hit big or I miss big. I like to live as big as I can."
George Herman Ruth

CHAPTER ONE

NIKKI

THIS LINGERIE SHOULD HAVE come with instructions. The black top criss-crossed across the front and back with several straps, which looked beyond cute on the model at the shop. Of course, at home, I'd managed to turn it into some sort of bondage get-up. It was supposed to be airy and light with skin showing through in an elegant tease. Instead, I appeared to have been trussed up and made to squeal like a pig.

"Damn!" I stripped it off my head and tried again.

"Nik, you okay in there?" Braden's voice filtered through the door.

"I'm good. You're really going to love it."

"I love you naked. Anything else is extra. I'm hard as a rock in here."

I rolled my eyes. "Just be patient."

"I'm patient." He groaned. "But my dick's not. How much longer?"

"Just a minute. Shush, momma's busy!"

Focus. Separating the strips of material, I slid the lingerie over my head, careful to put the front straps in front and the back in back. Once it was in place, I checked it in the mirror over the sink. Success. Something about just a little fabric always seemed sexier to me than full skin, though Braden would disagree. Ever since I'd moved in a month ago, he'd been trying to convince me that there should be a "home is where the clothes aren't" rule. Though I'd refused to strip

1

when I walked in the door every evening, he certainly did his best to make sure I was naked and beneath him as much as possible. And I didn't mind it one bit.

I smiled at myself in the mirror and primped my blonde curls. It was our six-month anniversary, so I wanted to do something extra memorable. Super spicy sexy-times was the logical choice. And the lingerie I'd picked definitely fit the bill. It was slinky, sexy, and super slutty—in other words, it was perfect.

All I needed to complete the look was the black thong.

"Nik, my balls are turning a beautiful blue out here. You should see them. No, actually you should taste them. Really get the blueberry flavor."

"Almost done!"

My feet slapped across the warm marble tile to the walk-in closet. I snagged the thong from the top of the hamper and gave myself another inspection in the full-length mirror along the back wall.

"What the fuck?" I stepped closer and glanced down to a single patch of blonde hair on my pussy. My usual waxing lady had been out earlier in the day, so my appointment had been with the aptly-named Helga. Her uni-brow was a thing of legend. But her waxing skills were not.

"No, no, no." I shook my head. The tuft of hair was along the right side, completely out of place. Not a landing strip, more of a crash site. It had to go.

Braden wouldn't care. Hell, he probably wouldn't even notice. But I wanted everything to be perfect for our anniversary. I could fix it. I darted back into the bathroom and yanked out a drawer in the wide vanity. Digging around, I seized the self-waxing strips I'd bought when I'd feared I was sprouting a mustache. Turned out it was just a bit of smudged gelato on my upper lip.

I skimmed the instructions. "Blah blah blah, skin irritation, discomfort blah. Rip strip IMMEDIATELY after applying or risk chemical burn blah blah." I set the box down and pulled out a pair of waxing strips, the adhesive parts stuck together.

Braden's laugh rolled through the door.

"What?" I called and warmed the wax strips between my palms.

"Easton sent me a pic of Kasey's face. She must have gotten trashed last night. He's drawn the most anatomically correct dick on her cheek, and it really looks like the tip's in her mouth. He put a caption: 'Kasey's First Blowie.' There's drool and everything."

Easton, Braden's best friend and teammate, had a sister who'd groped me countless times since the day we met. She was crude, hilarious, and beyond deserving of a deftly-drawn dick on the side of her face. I quirked a smile, but didn't laugh. I was on a mission, after all.

I pulled the wax strips apart and dashed back to the full-length mirror. Raising my right leg, I positioned it on one of the shelves along the side of the closet. The patch of hair mocked me. I peeled the strips apart, so that I had two, each of them sticky on one side. *This will be easy.*

I tried to put one of the strips down on top of the drawers, because I realized I only needed one to get the job done. But the thin plastic flipped up and it became stuck on the back of my fingers.

"Shit." I glanced to the strip in my free hand. If I put it down, it could get stuck, too, and then I'd have to start all over again. Instead, I spread my leg wider and smoothed the strip onto the patch of hair. It went on easy, and my skin tingled just a little. I tried to grab it with my right hand and hold the skin tight with my left, but the fingers on my right hand were glued together from the spare strip.

Shaking my head at myself in the mirror, I put my leg down, and the edge of the plastic strip affixed to my pussy poked into my thigh. I crab-walked back to the bathroom and held the wax-stripped hand under the warm water. It loosened enough to where I could pull it off, but it left a gooey residue on my fingers. I sniffed it. It definitely did not smell like the organic wax used at Madame Muff's House of

Hairlessness.

I turned the water to a hotter setting and tried again, but the goo didn't budge. I grabbed the yellow hand towel hanging next to my sink to try and wipe my fingers off. The towel got stuck, but with more than a little effort, I was able to scrape it across my fingers and wipe the gunk off. By that time, the hairy spot on my pussy was on fire.

"Nik, if you aren't out here and on my dick in sixty seconds, I'm going to come in there and get you."

"I'm coming."

I ran back to the mirror and hiked my leg.

"No, you aren't, not yet." Oh, God, his voice was getting closer.

"Just a minute."

"You don't have a minute."

"Braden!" I put my left fingers on the skin beside the strip, drawing it tight, and grabbed the plastic with my right. Taking a deep breath, I ripped it free.

I yelped. Searing pain radiated up my body, bringing tears to my eyes and sending me to my knees. "Oh no, oh no."

Braden's feet pounded the floor behind me, and he ran around to my front. I pressed one hand to the burning spot on my pussy.

"What is it? Are you okay?"

I whipped my head up to answer him, and his rock-hard cock poked me in the eye. I squeaked at the sting.

"Oh, shit!" Braden jumped away, but it was too late.

My eye watered, thanks to the jab from his cock. I fell back, one hand on my pussy, the other clapped over my eye. My cries were more of a yowl as Braden dropped to his knees next to me.

I rocked back and forth on the cool wood floor of the closet, tears streaming down to my ears.

"Nik, babe, I'm so sorry. Let me see it." He peeled my fingers from my face and examined my eye. I squinted at the closet light.

"It just looks a little red."

"Your cock goes in my pussy, not my eye." I choked out through the tears.

"I know, baby." He pulled me into a sitting position and held me against his chest. "It sure does."

I kept my hand over the angry spot of skin between my legs, too afraid to look at the damage I'd done.

"What's this?" He ran his hand down my arm and rested it on my thigh.

"I-I- Nothing."

He pulled me away and stared at me with his hazel eyes. "Come on, Nik. What happened? Let me see."

"No!" I clamped my legs together, but it didn't do much good. My hips were wide enough for me to have the thigh gap—usually a blessing, but at this point, more of a curse.

"Move your hand." He lowered his voice, the tone of command thrilling me and petrifying me all at once.

"It's fine. Just go back to bed—"

His brows pinched together until they formed a 'W'. "Nik, now."

I wiped my eyes with my free hand and peered down. Pulling my hand away, I cringed at the angry red patch left behind. There wasn't any hair, and barely any skin.

"Jeez, babe. What did you do to yourself?" He leaned over to inspect it, his face inches from my pussy, but not in a good way.

I began to cry more.

He leaned back up to my face and smoothed his thumbs along my cheeks, wiping my tears. "Does it hurt bad? I'm sorry. I've got some cortisone. It'll make it feel better in a hurry." He hopped to his feet and jogged to the bathroom, his muscled ass flexing with each step.

I wasn't crying because it hurt, though it did. I'd ruined our six-month anniversary over a patch of hair the size of a nickel. More tears flowed as Braden returned and dabbed some cream on my pussy—definitely not the sort of cream I'd envisioned for our night together.

When he was done, he tossed the tube of ointment on

the floor and scooped me into his arms. Before long, he'd laid me on the bed and pulled me to him.

"Don't cry, baby. I know it hurts."

"It's not that." I sniffled. "I mean, that hurts, but I've ruined our anniversary." I sobbed a little harder. Just hearing the words made it worse.

He shook against me, and I stopped crying for a moment to lift my head up to see what was wrong. A big grin spread across his face. He was laughing at me.

My sadness turned to anger. "Braden!" I beat on his chest, but he only laughed and pulled me closer.

"Don't be silly. Nothing is ruined. You're here with me where you belong, burned pussy and all." His laughter grew louder, breaking up his words.

The phone on his nightstand chimed again, Easton probably regaling him with some more dick drawing tales. I couldn't tell if I wanted to scratch Braden or kiss him. I dug my nails into his ribs and he tensed, but took it. He deserved it.

He stroked his hand through my hair as his other arm held me tight. His shaking subsided and he kissed the crown of my head. "I love you, Nik. As long as you're with me, we're good, okay? My balls can stay blue until tomorrow or whenever you're better. Maybe the blueberry taste will be even sweeter by then. I don't know."

I dug my nails in harder and then released him. His words were too mushy for me to stay mad. "I love you, too."

"I know." He sighed. "What did you even do to yourself down there?"

I nipped at his chest. "There was this little patch that the waxing lady missed, so I figured I'd get it myself—"

He started shaking again. My nails dug back into his side. "I'm sorry, Nik. Sorry. Continue. I won't laugh."

"Well, that's pretty much the end of it. I tried to make it perfect—"

"It was already perfect long before you went to get it waxed."

I snuggled into his chest. "Why do you always say the right thing?"

"Hmm, I think I usually say the wrong thing."

"Not to me." I draped my arm over his back and just let him hold me for a while. Our breathing evened out and the sting in my crotch began to fade.

"How does it feel now?" He ran his hand up and down my side.

"Better."

"Good. Want to see something to cheer you up?"

I snorted. "Kasey eating a dick?"

"You know me so well." He rolled onto his back and reached out with his tanned, muscled arm to snag his phone. Swiping across the screen, the image immediately popped up. He'd set it as his wallpaper.

"Easton really is an artist." The dick, hard and with a nice set of balls and pubic hair, was drawn along her cheek, the tip in her open, drooling mouth. I had to laugh. Kasey was smart, beautiful, and hated dick. "It's perfect."

My phone beeped, the notification light blinking blue. I sighed and reached for it. After all, my singed kitty wasn't getting any play tonight. It lit up when I grabbed it. There was a message from my mother.

"I'm typing back to him that he needs to add some conditioner or something on her face, like it's jizz, you know she'll really—"

"Oh my God!" I smiled and turned to Braden. He was still in the middle of typing his crude, juvenile, and admittedly funny conditioner idea to Easton. "Mom and Dad are having a dinner and they've invited us. *Both* of us."

My parents hadn't invited a boyfriend for dinner in years, likely because I'd never settled down with one guy. Not until Braden. Like everyone else, they thought he was just another man in my long career of cleat chasing. But he wasn't. Braden was something different, something special—the man I loved. Finally, Mom and Dad understood.

He stopped typing and swallowed hard. Laying his phone

7

on his chest, he ran a hand through his short chestnut brown hair. "So me meeting your parents, that's a good thing?"

I grinned and crawled on top of him, careful to keep my poisoned pussy patch from making contact. "It's the best thing. I can't wait to show you off." Leaning down, I kissed him. After a moment, he returned it. Braden was a lot of things—star athlete, decent dresser, funny, smart, hot as fuck—but far and away his best attribute was his kissing ability. You've never been kissed until you've been kissed by Braden Bradford. And that's too bad, because he only kisses *me*.

His tongue swooped inside my mouth, and he put a hand at the back of my neck, directing the kiss. I was more than happy to be turned whichever way suited him. I moaned into his mouth, my pussy heating up despite the spot of scorched earth. He ran his other hand to my ass, but when he pushed me down against his cock, I squeaked at the sting and pulled away.

"Shit, I'm sorry. I forgot because—" he glanced down to his raging erection "—he made me forget."

I rolled off and sat next to him. "It's okay."

He put both hands to his temples, his biceps flexing. "So, your parents?"

"Yes." I lay down and snuggled into his side. "They'll love you."

"You sure?"

"More than sure. Now, go to sleep. This pussy will feel better in the morning, and I want you to make it feel even better. Got me?"

His lips curled in a devious smile as he tossed his phone back to the nightstand next to mine. "Yes, ma'am."

"And don't worry." I yawned. "My father's only ever shot one of my boyfriends."

CHAPTER TWO

BRADEN

I RAN THE SHOW. I faced the opposite direction of all the other players, and I was the only one that had a view of the entire field. I was the leader—the goddamn shot caller, and these whores needed to get their shit together.

"Time!" I held my hand up to the ump as the crowd fell nearly silent.

We were up one run, with a runner on first in the top of the ninth, two outs. Gladden was on the mound. I shook my head. *Fucking rookies.* He'd thrown a hell of a game so far, but he was showing all the signs of fatigue—leaving pitches up in the zone, arm hanging, loss of velocity.

I trotted out toward the mound while the low hum of the stadium encircled me. Heat from the sun beat down on my gear, trapping the humid warmth beneath my jersey. It was hot as fuck for a September evening.

When I reached the mound, I looked out to see the giant pussy bag known as Easton Holliday warming up in the pen beyond right field. I turned my gaze back to Gladden and pried the catcher's helmet from my head. "You're done. Huh?"

His head dropped, and he scuffed his cleat in the dirt. When he met my eyes again, I could tell he knew it was time to hand the ball over.

"It's no biggie, man. Just let me know so we can fucking win this shit for you. Don't be a hero." I looked over to the opposing dugout. Their clean-up hitter was up next. *Fuck.*

9

"Yeah, man. I'm spent." He lifted his hat and wiped his brow with his sleeve.

I glanced to Coach in the dugout, and the old crotchety bastard started up the steps and toward the field. Coach and I liked to joke around. But on the field it was all business. He knew the look.

Coach made his way toward us, lightly dragging his foot over the chalk line on the way just to fuck it up a little. *Respect.* I turned to Gladden. "You did good, kid. Hold your head up when all these peckerdicks cheer for you. Got me?" I cracked a smile.

He grinned. "Thanks, B."

"Good game, Gladden. Let E mop up for you." Coach stopped a few feet away and held out his hand for the ball. Gladden placed it in his palm, and the stadium thundered as he walked to the dugout.

I looked out to right field and Andre the Dickless Giant was mowing down the grass with his cleats as he jogged out toward us.

"Glad he's on our side," Coach said.

I glanced over to Coach and smirked. "Nice observation. Thank God we have someone like you around, sir. To impart these gold nuggets of wisdom."

His head slowly turned until his eyes met mine. "Suck my dick." His words were a low whisper, almost like a sigh.

I did my best not to break character, but it wasn't easy. I glared back and mumbled. "I wouldn't suck your dick with Easton's mouth. And I'd love to make him suck a dick. A whole factory of fucking dicks, Coach. We're talking Costco in bulk dicks here."

The corners of his lips curled up. Forty-five thousand people surrounded us, and we still behaved like twelve-year-olds.

He slapped the ball in my mitt. "Don't fuck it up, Braden." He turned and headed toward the dugout.

"Yeah. Yeah. Go sit on your fat ass and let us make you look good."

"Plan on it," he called over his shoulder.

Jesus, how the fuck could he hear me?

I turned around, and Easton was right behind me, staring me down from above, *Children of the Corn* style. "Jesus." I shuddered.

He laughed. "Can I have the ball, princess?"

"What'd I tell you about sneaking up on me like that, bitch?" I handed him the ball.

"Sorry not sorry. Can I go to work now?" E adjusted his cap.

I reached down and latched a shin guard that had come undone. "Yeah, man. You know the drill with this cunt." I nodded toward their hitter. "Chases low and away."

"I'm on it." E tapped his glove on mine.

I trotted back behind home plate. Once there, I held up my pinky and index finger to everyone. "Two down. Focus on the hitter! Runners don't mean shit."

I had to tell them even the simplest of things, because they would constantly forget.

I squatted down behind the plate, my knees popping and cracking just like every other catcher's. Leading the team had always been hard on the knees.

Easton tossed a few warmup pitches. Once finished, I glanced over to the net. Nikki, Kyrie, and Kasey were in their usual seats. Nikki blew me a kiss, and I smiled. Kyrie had finally put her fucking Kindle down and was staring out at Easton. Kasey scowled at me, made a jerk-off motion, and flung ghost jizz in my direction.

I caught it and rubbed it into my chest protector, obviously.

Focus.

The big batter next to me dug his cleat into the dirt and twisted his foot as if he were squashing an imaginary bug.

Show me the other foot, butternuts.

He followed my instructions like a good little bitch and brought his front foot to rest slightly angled out to left field.

He's sitting on fastball.

I called for a slider away, and Easton shook me off like a Neanderthal, so I threw it down again. He came set, and checked the runners. At the last moment, I slid to the outside corner like a goddamn ninja and flipped up my glove to give him a target.

He exploded toward me. I saw the familiar dot on the ball from the rotation of the slider and caught it six inches off the plate. The idiot to my left whiffed hard enough to start a typhoon on the other side of the world.

I laughed and tossed the ball back to Easton. "That a kid. Listen to Daddy back here. He knows what's up."

"The fuck you laughing at, prick?" The big dummy of a hitter stared down at me.

"A goddamn circus clown. What do you think?" I chuckled again and nodded at him.

"Keep it clean, boys. Let's play ball." Pussy-ass umpires always ruined all the shit-talking fun.

"Yes, sir." I didn't sound sarcastic at all in my reply.

I lifted my mask to wipe beads of sweat and dirt that quickly turned to some kind of mud concoction on my face.

Easton stalked back up to the rubber, and I looked over at bitch boy's feet. The hitter crowded up on the plate with his front toe turned in.

Ohh, bad mistake motherfucker.

"Wouldn't crowd homeboy's plate. He ain't like it." I flattened my right palm in the dirt and moved it back and forth, using the dry earth to soak up some of the sweat from my palm.

"Fuck you, Braden. This is *my* plate." He waved the bat back and forth at Easton.

"You were warned."

Easton did appear menacing for such a big teddy bear. His glove was up, covering his face, and his hat was pulled down so that I could only see his eyes. But, I knew he was smiling up a shit storm under the glove when I called for the fastball inside.

I rocked back to my heels and braced myself for it as he

went into his motions. The big ox could throw hard as fuck.

His arm was a whirlwind and the ball buzzed before exploding into my glove, right behind where the batter once stood. I looked over at him, lying in the dirt on his back.

"Told ya." I winked.

The asshole jumped to his feet and kicked his big clown foot at the ground, roiling up a dirt cloud as he stared Easton down.

"Make a move. I'm right here. Stay off my goddamn plate." Easton held his glove up, signaling for me to get the ball back to him.

I happily obliged. "I told his ass, E. He don't listen."

"That's a warning for all three of you. Keep it up, and your asses are gone." The ump wagged a finger at me. It was kind of cute.

"Yes, sir." I grinned.

Easton walked back up to the mound. I looked over to my man's legs wobbling like jello, foot pointed out to left field again.

He's fucked.

I called for the slider away, and big boy on the mound learned his lesson and nodded. He came set and threw the pitch. This one started down the middle and broke to the outside corner.

The batter swung and got a tiny piece of the ball with the tip of the bat. The ball rolled into the grass about ten feet away and came to rest.

"You knocked the shit out of that one." I chuckled.

"Fuck you. Stop talking to me." He beat the end of the bat on his cleat as the crowd stood. Two strikes, two outs, game on the line. They were definitely amped up for the payoff pitch.

"God, so sensitive. Fine." I mocked him in a falsetto. It was all too easy to get into a hitter's head.

The cheers of the crowd grew to a deafening roar as Easton took the bump, ready to finish this guy the fuck off.

Don't hang that shit again, E. Hit your spots.

The hitter dug in, and I called for the slider way out. Might as well make him look extra stupid on national TV for his wife and mother to see.

When Easton started to deliver I kicked my leg out in true acrobat fashion and set up off the plate. The pitch was perfect. Cock boy never had a chance. It came in hard and broke away at the last second as he blew down every tree in the city trying to hit it. The ball slammed into my glove.

"Haaah!" The umpire got into it, even though there was no need since the guy swung.

Fuck it. Let him have his moment in the sun.

I fist-pumped and turned to the hitter, holding up my glove to show him the ball. "Looking for this, pussyboy?" I laughed as I strolled out and bumped gloves with Easton. The rest of the team followed, and we all slapped fives and said congratulations. We were on a roll, and Easton had been unhittable ever since getting serious with the growing-in-popularity Kyrie Kent.

With this win, we'd be on our way to the playoffs, and after that, anything was possible—the pennant, the World Series, maybe even the Gryffindor House Cup.

"You were great, babe!" Nik's tits pressed against my chest while she kissed me. My Violet Beauregard blueberry balls yearned for a release.

"She ready to go?" I whispered in her ear.

"She is off the disabled list and ready for cock." Nik leaned back and stared at me.

"Good. He misses you, you know?" I glanced to the tent forming in my jeans.

"I know, baby. I sure do. I missed him too." She brushed her ass against my dick as she turned to say hi to everyone else.

I glanced around the bar. It was the same place where Easton nearly destroyed Sean's face. Ahh, the memories. I nudged Easton. "Want to go grab a couple pitchers of Smithwicks?"

"Yep." He turned on his heel, and we strode toward the bar.

I leaned down and propped my elbows on the smooth wood surface. The difference in weight on my knees made me wince a little.

"Knees?" Easton looked down at my legs.

"They'll be fine. Some of us have to do real work. Not fuck off like pitchers and shag flies all day." I smirked.

"Yeah, you do a lot of work on your knees, I hear. Surprised they lasted this long." He did that thing where he pretended to jerk an imaginary dick near his mouth and stuck his tongue in his cheek in rhythm.

"It's not my fault your mom grabs me by the hair and bucks on my face like she's riding a prized bull. Shit is like licking sandpaper." I looked up at him and tried to keep a straight face.

A vein bulged in his neck. I shrugged it off. He started it. Crude humor was my thing. If he didn't like it, he could eat a bag of dicks.

"Really?" He turned to the bartender and ordered two pitchers.

Why let the fun stop? "Really, man. It's like the Sahara down there. I'll find the oasis one day I suppose. The struggle is real."

While E worked up his next comeback, I reached out and snagged a coaster and began picking at the edges.

Instead of blasting me with a well-deserved insult, he put a hand on my shoulder. "Everything okay?"

I scoffed and forced myself to leave the coaster alone. He'd picked up on my tell. "Yeah, man. I'm good."

"Braden, look at me."

Fuck. I turned my head and whistled. Talking things out was for chicks. Not me.

15

"What's up?" He burned a hole in the side of my head with his stare.

"It's nothing, man. Don't sweat it." I turned to him, hoping he'd leave it alone.

"Tell me what's up. You're acting weird."

I sighed. There was no getting rid of him. "It's just some bullshit with Nik's parents. Got me a little stressed. It's nothing."

He grinned. "Meeting the parents, huh? You guys pregnant?" He laughed at his own joke like a rookie.

I flashed him my best you're-a-fucking-idiot look.

"So what, man? You'll be fine." He handed some money to the bartender.

"I know. I mean—umm—it's just different with her. And she's super excited about it. Not making shit easier. Know what I mean?" I grabbed one of the pitchers of beer.

"Just nerves. You'll ace the parent test. You're you, after all." He looked me up and down. "People like you. You're fine."

I looked over at Nik, her perfect body hugged by her tight jeans and Ravens t-shirt that she had bedazzled up with my number. Classic Nik style. "I love her, man. Like bad. I don't want to fuck it up. I know they'll be uppity. She comes from money and shit."

"Just be yourself. If they hate you, then it's because they already do. And nothing you could do would change that. Trust me."

We started toward the table.

"I guess." I shrugged, but kept the pitcher steady, because spilling beer was a crime against humanity.

"It's about time you two dick shits brought the beer. You finish whitewashing his tonsils, Braden? We all know Easton is a catcher at heart." Kasey snickered.

"Keep it up, lil sis. Heard you sucked off a Sharpie hog last night." I grinned at Kasey as her cheeks grew a slight pink.

"Laugh it up, twinkle titties. I'll never suck a dick. *Ever!*"

Kyrie and Nik giggled. Kasey swiped the pitcher from my hand and filled her glass.

Easton looked over at Nik then back to me. "Don't be a pussy. It's time to shit or get off the pot."

CHAPTER THREE

NIKKI

"… AND THAT'S WHY I'LL never do my own waxing ever again." I finished my tale of woe with a flourish of my hands and a satisfied smile on my face. I should have been an actress or a motivational speaker.

Kyrie stared at me from across the table, her mouth slightly agape. The rest of the faces around the table were littered with a variety of expressions—all could have been classified in the 'aghast' category.

"Thank you for that fascinating trip into your juvenile psyche and utter inability to follow simple instructions." Graciela Froggart peered over her cat eye glasses, displeasure written in the lines around her eyes and the downturn of her lips. "I would ask if there was a point, but I believe we've all learned that, with you, the answer would be no." She surveyed the conference table, packed with ten editors and their assistants. "Let's move on to the actual business of the day—"

"Actually, I was thinking maybe we should do a piece on proper pussy haircare? Err, I mean *vagina*. Because that's what doctors call it." I cleared my throat. "Anyway, every woman gets waxed or at the very least, trims. Maybe we could give tips on how to choose the right waxing boutique or what waxes are the best for your skin if you're a do-it-yourselfer." I chanced a glance at Kyrie. Her dark eyebrows popped up a little, as if surprised I actually followed through with an article idea.

19

"Well, Nikki …" Graciela twirled her pen in her bony fingers and stared down her nose at me. "I think … Yes, I do think that would actually be a nice piece to put in our beauty section. Have you discussed this with Kyrie? I'll expect her to direct your efforts. That's the only way I'll entertain such an article from you." She stopped twirling the pen and used it to point at me. "But keep it classy. No shenanigans. If I see the word 'pussy' or—" she closed her eyes and wrinkled her nose with disdain "—'cunt' anywhere in it, I'll trash it right off. Got me?"

A thrill went through me at the prospect of my first real assignment. "Right. It will be up to the *Style and Substance* standard. I promise. No pussies, cunts, clams, cooches, gashes, slashes, twats, snatches—"

Graciela held up her hand. "I think we quite get it now, Nikki. Thank you for your contribution. I do believe I've had enough from Kyrie's department for the day. Now, let's talk fashion …" She continued down the row of editors, asking about articles on clothing and accessories.

I couldn't contain my grin, and Kyrie kept sneaking glances at me. She wanted to frown, but I could see the laughter in her eyes. This was my first chance to really show what I was capable of. Ever since we'd moved up to *Style and Substance* a few months ago, I'd been stuck with dealing with disputes over ad placement and reviewing boring ad copy.

I didn't want to do the grunt work anymore. My dream was to be a senior editor, someone who ran an entire section of a magazine. Maybe the dream wouldn't happen at *Style and Substance*, but I knew I'd get there eventually. I just had to keep working, keep doing my best, and—most importantly—never sacrifice who I was to fit into someone else's mold. As long as I stayed true to myself, my dream would come true.

This was just the beginning. When Graciela agreed to let me do my own thing, my heart skipped a beat and a blush crept over my skin. I wanted to shine here, to work my way up to editor instead of editorial assistant. With Kyrie's support, I knew I could make it happen. I wouldn't waste this chance.

After the meeting, I scurried to my office. It was more like a closet, but I didn't mind. At least I had a door. That was more than I ever had when I was at *Teen Sparkle*. My small desk took up most of the windowless room, but I'd decorated with brash art and even managed to wedge in a tiny bench for visitors to sit on. It was my little slice of home away from home. Working for Kyrie, my best friend, made it even more enjoyable.

I walked in, sank down at my desk, and leaned my head back against the leather chair. I may have even squeed a little.

"Way to go in there." Kyrie perched her curvy ass on the edge of my desk. "Just out of curiosity, how many more words for pussy were you going to throw out?"

"Want me to keep on impressing you? I can always go with a nice hatchet wound or a poon, beaver, furburger." I met her green gaze, loving it when they widened with each word I came up with.

Kyrie shook her head and laughed. "You are ridiculous."

"You love me."

"I do." She nodded, still smiling, and tucked a stray wisp of brown hair behind her ear. "Is this new?" She pointed at my strapless green dress. "I love it. Too bad my tits are way too big to go strapless."

I patted my chest. "Not a problem with me." I'd always been petite. With my blonde hair, clear skin, and light brown eyes, my mother tried to get me into modeling, but I was always too short to land any big photo shoots.

"They're as perky as the day is long. I'm jealous." She sighed and ran her hands down her sides, highlighting her hourglass figure.

I wanted to throw my stapler at her. "Show off. And if I remember correctly, the last time I saw your big squishies, the nips were still pointing north, so I'm pretty sure you could go strapless if you wanted to."

"Maybe, but I'd probably get written up for indecent

exposure."

I waved her words away as if they were an irritating gnat. "Days without a reprimand aren't worth living."

"Oh, Nik, what am I going to do with you?" She stood to leave. "I just wanted to stop by and congratulate you. I'm proud, and I can't wait to see what you come up with."

I slapped her thigh. "Put that fine ass back on my desk. I've got news."

A creaking wheel noise echoed through the hall. I knew the sound. I pretended to reach for my notepad and knocked it off my desk and onto the floor at Kyrie's feet. Like a dutiful friend, she bent over to pick it up. Right then, Grady pushed past with the mail cart.

He stopped, his pervy eyes growing huge as he got a good look at Kyrie's ass. Her skirt was short enough for me to wonder if he got a view of panties. When he reached down to adjust himself in his pants, my hypothesis was proven accurate.

"Here." Kyrie straightened and handed me my notepad, then followed my gaze to the door. "Grady, get the fuck out of here!"

"Y-yes, ma'am." Grady took off with his cart, but seconds later a crash sounded from down the hall. He must have run into the nearest cubicle.

I howled with laughter. Thank God that creeper followed us over to *Style and Substance*. His stalker ways always managed to lighten my day.

"You did that on purpose." Kyrie, her cheeks red and her eyes flashing, grabbed a lock of my hair and yanked.

"I had that coming." I couldn't contain my laughter. "Just like Grady's going to be coming all over your imaginary ass in the men's room in about five minutes." That comment got me another, harder hair pull.

"I'm leaving." She huffed and turned for the door.

"No, don't go. I'm sorry." I grabbed her hand and stowed my giggles, though I had to push the image of Grady's bugged-out eyes from my mind to do it.

She glowered. "You're going to regret all this when I'm at the bottom of Grady's well rubbing lotion on my skin."

I gave her my most earnest look. "You have to do it, or else you'll get the hose again."

"Dammit, Nikki." She fought a smile, but her lips won and she finally let out a laugh. "You are the fucking worst. You know that?"

"I do. I think you tell me about once a day. Now sit down. I'm being serious. I have real, actual news."

She dutifully reclaimed her perch, though her eyes had a wary glint. "Good news? Bad news? What news?"

"Great news!"

"That's my favorite kind." She crossed her legs at the knee. "Hit me."

"Well, you know how my parents moved back from Florida two months ago?"

She nodded. "Yeah, did they sell the beach house?"

I rolled my eyes. "Are you kidding? No. They're having a major renovation, so they've come back to the estate for a few months. As soon as it gets cold, they'll be flying south again for the winter."

My parents had inherited more money than they knew what to do with. I'd learned long ago that vast sums of money allow people to be their real selves. They go about life completely differently than normal humans. My parents were a prime example. They'd returned to the city because of what they'd termed a "monumental hardship." This "hardship" was the scent of Vietnamese food. They'd hired a new housekeeper at the beach house, but didn't like the smell of what she cooked in her own personal kitchen in the servants' wing of the house. So, they decided the only wise thing to do was buy the beach cottage next door, knock it down, and build a separate servants' home. Totally logical to people like my parents, but batshit crazy to the normal people of the world.

"So, if they aren't back for good, what's the news?"

"They want to meet Braden!" My voice was too loud for

the office environment, but I didn't care. "I can't wait for them to meet him. They are going to love him."

Kyrie smiled but crossed her arms, pushing her boobs up and straining the button on her white cardigan. "Does Braden know?"

"Yeah." I fidgeted in my seat. The chemical burn on my pussy had entered the itching stage of healing.

"Is he excited?" She raised a brow.

"Well, not as excited as I am—"

She sighed. "Oh, Nik. Nobody gets as excited as you do. That's a given."

"I know, but I think he wants to meet them. He didn't say no or anything. We're supposed to go to their house for dinner this weekend. I can already imagine him wowing my dad and flirting with my mom, and oh my God, it's going to be perfect." My words ran together in a jumble of excitement.

"Just make sure he's comfortable with it. Boys are weird about meeting parents. And sometimes parents, not just yours, get overly protective. But yours … I can see Catherine and John playing good cop, bad cop."

I wrinkled my nose. "I don't want to hear about my parents' perverted sex games, you deviant."

She held my gaze and ignored my attempt to deflect. "You know what I mean."

I shrugged. "Just because that one time my father shot my boyfriend when they were out hunting. I mean, it was an accident, and Clay didn't die or anything."

"Yeah, but where did he get shot?"

I looked away and chewed my lip. "In the groin."

She kicked my leg with her black pump. "In the *dick*. Have you told Braden about that?"

"Ow!" I rubbed my knee. "I mentioned it in passing. Said it was a hunting accident."

"Did he buy it?" She pulled a strand of dark hair between her teeth and bit down.

She must have been really worried. She didn't do the

hair-biting move unless something had her riled up.

"Look, they will love Braden because I love him, okay? Don't worry so much. And I won't let him go hunting with Dad, so none of that will be an issue." Despite my words, worry swirled in my stomach. Was she right? Had I underestimated the pressure this situation would put on Braden and me?

"What about Vanessa and Ben?"

"Vanessa's away at school, and Ben might show up." My little sister was the sweetest soul in the world, and my older brother wasn't far behind. If a black sheep was allowed in the Graves family, I was it.

Even so, my parents had always been polite to my boyfriends. Except that one incident in the woods, they had never openly declared war against any of my dating choices. Braden was my first long-term relationship since college, so surely they would realize it was serious.

I tapped my index finger on my thigh. Come to think of it, I *had* failed to mention we were living together. And by 'failed to mention,' I meant 'intentionally did not mention.' Not that I was ashamed of Braden, but I didn't want to rock the boat with my parents. They wouldn't be too pleased about me shacking up with a baseball player they'd never met. But I hadn't lied to them or anything. I just hadn't mentioned it. That was different, wasn't it?

Kyrie put a hand on my shoulder and squeezed, drawing me from my thoughts. "I'm sure everything will be fine. It has to be, right?"

"Right." I nodded, though I wasn't quite so sure anymore.

She stood and smoothed down her plum skirt. "Now, let's get to work. When are you going to start on the waxing article?"

I shook off the worrisome thoughts and grinned at her. "No time like the present. So, when was the last time you had your cooter waxed?"

CHAPTER FOUR
BRADEN

RAUCOUS CHEERS MORPHED INTO a steady roar from the crowd as Cox slid into third. I swung my bat in the on-deck circle to the right of home plate.

"Hell yeah, kid!" I yelled.

Cox popped up on third and fist-bumped our assistant coach before brushing the dirt from his uniform. The frenzy continued in the stands. I turned my gaze out to second base where Hamilton stood after driving a double to the right centerfield wall. "Atta boy, Ham Chops!"

He stared at me with a bright-white, toothy smile and pounded his chest twice with his fist. I returned the gesture.

I strode up to the plate from the on-deck circle, and the thunderous applause grew louder as my name rang out over the speakers. Pendleton had struck out to start off the inning, but now we had two runners in scoring position with one out. Momentum was on our side. Adrenaline pumped through my veins as I looked up to the scoreboard—a giant picture of my face covered half of it—to verify the scenario. We were down three to two in the bottom of the ninth.

I couldn't help but notice my batting average taunting me underneath my pretty face.

.247

It was fifty points lower than the numbers I usually put up each year. The breaks hadn't gone my way at all this season, and those three little numbers were all that the people in the front office cared about. Not leadership, or heart. Fucking numbers.

Focus, goddamn it.

I slapped the hard lumber into my palm, and inhaled a huge breath through my nose. Hot dogs, beer, and fresh cut bermuda flooded my nostrils. The smell of the ballpark was heaven.

I propped the bat between my legs and scooped a pile of fresh dirt into my hands, before rubbing them together. I clapped a couple of times, sending a cloud of dirt swirling out toward the mound, and grabbed the handle of my bat. Gripping it hard, I squeezed the wood tight in my palms, gaining the necessary friction to go to work.

Fuck the numbers. Get your teammates a win.

"Let's go, B. Light his ass up," hollered Easton.

E and the others were in my peripheral vision, leaning on the barrier in front of the dugout. I kept my focus on the mound. Glaring at the pitcher, I dug in with my right foot as the cheers of the stadium turned to pandemonium.

"Time!" The ump threw up his hands, cutting off all the energy that had built inside of me moments before.

What the fuck?

I shot a glance to the opposing dugout as their fat fuck manager waddled his ass onto the field. *Cunt.*

I stepped out of the box, my concentration now broken, and walked toward our dugout. I headed right for Coach.

"Fucker is going to bring in Martinez. He's trying to ice me." I glared at the old man.

"Looks like it's working. Get your fucking head in it." His eyes bore into my skull.

He was right.

"Yes, sir."

"Use your brain, son. It's how you've always stayed a step ahead of everyone. You're smart. Quit sitting on your heels and reacting to everything. It's a chess game. You have to be thinking three moves ahead." His hands went to his hips.

Martinez jogged out from the left field bullpen. He was a monster. Six foot six and built like a brick shithouse, but with a gut. He damn near threw as hard as E, but didn't have the same quality of secondary pitches.

I nodded to Coach. "He'll want to get ahead in the count."

"Good. Now you're being a fucking ballplayer. Go on." His lips curled up the slightest bit at the corners.

What sounded like a gunshot shook me from my concentration once more. I turned to see the catcher shake his glove hand like it was hot and toss the ball back to Martinez.

"Fucking guy can bring it." Coach glared.

"Alright. Fine. Let's see." I looked up and then back to Coach. "He'll want to work ahead. His curveball is shit. So I need to sit on first pitch fastball. It'll be the best pitch I get to hit."

"Exactly. You're a catcher. Use it to your advantage. Think in reverse. What would you do if you were catching Martinez right now? That's how you have to think, son. It ain't rocket science."

"I hope not. You'd be way out of your fucking element." I grinned.

Coach smiled. "You little shit. Go win the fucking game already."

"Done." I called over my shoulder.

"Batter!" The ump called for me and pointed to the batter's box.

I strode back up to the plate as I caught Martinez smiling at me.

I'm going to fuck you up, fat boy.

Visualization was the key to success. I don't know why it worked, but it did. Over and over I pictured the pitch, and me driving it right back at Martinez's ugly-ass face.

"Come on, baby! You got this." Nik's high, clear voice pierced through the ocean of noise.

I turned to where the girls usually sat. All three of them were on their feet, waiting in anticipation. Nikki smiled and blew me a kiss.

Anxiety coursed through my veins, as sure as the energy from the fans rumbled through the stadium.

Her excitement reminded me of how happy she'd been about the dinner at her parents' house. I glanced up to the scoreboard, but was confronted with the damn .247 again. Shitty batting average, dinner with the parents—I couldn't win. I was a hot fucking mess.

"Focus, son!"

Coach's voice. It was like he lived in my head. I regained my focus.

I held up a hand to the umpire and dug my back foot into the batter's box dirt like I was staking claim on my territory. When I dropped my hand to signal I was ready, I planted my front foot in and stared out at chubby fucknuts.

You got this shit.

I played the perfect scenario in my mind one more time—Martinez starting with a fastball, and me decapitating him with a shot up the middle.

I looked up and everything else faded. It was me and him, and only one of us would win.

Fastball. Fastball.

I twirled the bat in small circles behind my head as he nodded to the catcher and came set.

Loose hands. Fastball.

I relaxed my grip. The big bastard kicked his leg high and hard as I rocked my weight to my back foot. As soon as he let go, I knew it was my pitch.

I swung so hard I nearly came out of my cleats.

As soon as I connected I knew I was money, because I didn't feel a thing. The ball connected with the sweet spot and rocketed off the bat toward the left field gap.

I dropped my bat and sprinted toward first as the crowd came alive around me, and my feet pounded on the dirt. I glanced at Cox, who represented the tying run, jogging from third toward home. Hamilton was flying from second to third, trying to score the winning run.

I glanced to left field as I was rounding first, just in time to see the fielder lay out and make a catch that was destined to be on Plays of the Week in a matter of hours.

No! Fuck!

It was like a sack of rocks landed on my chest. Cox and Hamilton hurried back to their respective bases as the left fielder hopped up to his feet. All noise from the crowd ceased as I came to a screeching halt in the base path.

I clutched the top of my helmet with both hands and arched my back, staring momentarily up at the inky night, praying it was a bad dream. How the fuck did he make that catch? It was my shit luck. All damn season. I'd let the guys down again.

There's no time for pity, Braden. You're a goddamn leader. Act like one.

I held my head high and sprinted back to the dugout like I always did, whether I hit a homerun or struck out. It was classy, and set an example for my teammates. When I ran past first base, I turned to our new rookie who walked to the plate. He was eyeing my reaction.

I clapped my hands together and grinned at him. "Let's go. He ain't got shit." I tossed a grin to the sumo-looking motherfucker on the mound who was smiling at me. "Keep cheesing, dickhead! You're about to get lit the fuck up again."

I turned back to rookie bitch who now had a look of confidence on his face. He strode to the plate with a purpose. "You got this shit, kid."

When I reached the dugout, Coach beamed like I'd actually won the game for us. I still wanted to go straight to the clubhouse and destroy a few things, or maybe just have a pussy style ugly cry in the corner. Not a chance though. My boys needed me, whether I was at the plate or not.

Coach smacked me on the ass as I ran down the stairs. "Bad break. We're still in it."

I shoved my bat back into the rack and tossed my helmet up into my cubby.

Easton was leaning on the rail with the guys, and I made

my way up next to him to cheer on the rook. I'd let us down, but I could damn sure do my best to help another brother get us the win.

"You literally cannot catch a fucking break." He slapped the rail, then reconsidered. "Well, I mean you *can* catch one. Fuck it, you know what I mean."

It got a chuckle out of me. "It's the goddamn baseball gods. They have it in for me. What do you do?" I shrugged.

He spit some sunflower seed shells out onto the emerald grass in front of us. "Indeed. They are being mighty cunty to you. Don't sweat it, man. They're moody fucks. They'll come around. But rook up there doesn't have a chance."

I frogged him on his non-pitching shoulder. "Don't say that shit, bitch. You know better than that." I glared.

E scowled for a second, and then he dropped his gaze. "Sorry, man."

"Don't apologize to me. Pick up your teammate."

E broke into laughter momentarily, and then turned his stare up to rook.

"Rip his fucking tits!" E hollered, his hand half-cupped around his mouth.

"That's better." I turned back to watch rook most likely fail as Easton originally predicted. But I wouldn't have that kind of negative talk in my fucking dugout. Not a chance.

Our obesity-laden insults sliced through the air as Martinez kicked his leg. He fired the ball into home.

Crack!

Any ballplayer worth a shit knew the sound. I could've had my eyes closed and known that ball was destined for the outfield bleachers.

Rook dropped the bat and started toward first, his head craned to stare at the ball in flight. All of us in the dugout watched as if it were in slow motion. The ball shot into the stands. A brief melee ensued about twenty rows up in left field as the ball landed amidst a roiling sea of faces and hands.

Everything stilled for a split second before a rumbling

built around us, shaking the stadium. The players in the dugout erupted. Rook fist-pumped rounding first base as the disgraced pitcher sauntered off the field, his face buried in his glove.

Hah! You fat sack of dicks!

The dugout looked like a mosh pit as we all shoved our way out onto the field to go tackle the rook. When he turned to trot back after watching the ball fly over the wall, his eyes went from 'excited' to 'scared shitless' in an instant. I couldn't blame him. There was a herd of big motherfuckers storming his way, and he was about to end up underneath them.

He finally gave in, and held his arms out wide as we tackled him. Hands, arms, legs, dicks, asses—it was all a blur as everyone tried to make their way to him and slap at his helmet.

After a few moments, the dust settled. We wrapped up our celebratory antics and headed back toward the clubhouse. Rook walked over to me. I faked a huge smile at him, knowing it should've been me. But wasn't that what being a captain was about? Putting everyone else ahead of yourself? I needed to be happy for him, build his confidence.

"I wouldn't have done that without you, you know?"

"Bullshit." My smile disappeared, and I tried to walk past him.

He grabbed my forearm and squeezed. Usually, it would cost a fucking rookie some hazing, but this kid was all amped up on adrenaline and endorphins, so I let it slide.

"I mean it, man. Thank you." His grip tightened on my arm.

I smacked his hand away and stood nose to nose with him.

The fear returned to his eyes.

"Don't you ever fucking doubt your shit. You don't need me to hit homeruns. You need to believe *you* can hit homeruns. You're a bad motherfucker. Now you walk over to that hot as fuck reporter that's waiting to interview you, act like that homerun was business as usual, and then you take her home and make her scream your goddamn name against the wall while you pound that shit out from behind. Got me, rook?" I glared into his eyes.

"Got it, Cap." He smiled and headed toward the reporter.

"Hey, kid."

He turned around. "Yeah, Cap?"

"You did good tonight. Enjoy it. Because tomorrow it doesn't mean a fucking thing."

He tipped the bill of his helmet at me and continued toward the camera crew.

I glanced out to the crowd and saw Kyrie and Kasey still replaying the homerun and ensuing craziness. It looked like Kasey was trying to grip Kyrie's hips from behind and show her how to swing a bat. Kase winked at me and I shook my head. *Clever perv.*

I gave Nik a wave and another smile. She grinned at me the same way she did when she broke the news of the dinner with her parents. Two days, and I would be face to face with her family. If my luck held, they'd run me out of their home and forbid Nik from seeing me again. I almost tripped over my own damn feet at the thought of losing her.

Coach was waiting for me at the clubhouse steps. "Good game tonight, son."

"Sure." I nodded and tamped down the rising flood of worry.

"You were at your best. I'm fucking proud of you." His face wrinkled with a grin.

"Yeah, I guess. I could've done more at the plate. Head wasn't fully in it."

"I wasn't talking about the way you played. I was talking about just now." He nodded to the rook being interviewed and then headed into the clubhouse.

"Thanks, Coach." I would always put my shit aside on the field for the sake of the team, but that didn't mean I wouldn't take it home with me. I suspect Coach knew that, but it didn't matter as long as I didn't bring it back on the field.

I sat there for a few moments with my thoughts. Everything I was up against played through my mind—letting the guys down on the field, meeting Nik's parents, the sub-par stats I'd put up so far this season.

When I finally walked into the clubhouse, I noticed Coach on the phone in his office. His mood was all off. It looked like he was yelling, but I couldn't make out anything with all the celebration among the players and coaches.

After a few minutes he slammed the phone down so hard he may have shattered it.

I started toward E when Coach stepped into the door frame of his office. "Braden." His voice was loud and insistent.

I popped my head up, trying to see over the smiling players. "Yeah?"

His words went from angry to a somber note. "Need a word, son."

What in the hell? "On my way."

I'd usually have thought he was calling me to his office to make fun of me, but there was something about his voice, his face. I dug my nails into my palms at the thought of that phone call.

I strode over to Coach. "What's up?"

His face paled. "Come in. We need to chat. Close the door behind you."

"Yes, sir." A million knives dug into my stomach.

I took a step into his office, and he went back to his chair behind his desk. "The door, son." He glanced to the guys celebrating behind me.

Fuck me. This isn't good.

I turned around and grabbed the door knob, pulling it shut. I'd never prayed for anything in my entire life—but in that moment, I prayed today wasn't my last day on the diamond.

CHAPTER FIVE

NIKKI

THE MOMENT BRADEN APPEARED in the bar's doorway, I ran to him and jumped into his arms. I was worried he'd be upset about his almost-homerun, but he'd smiled at me from the field. So maybe it wasn't so bad after all?

He hugged me, and I buried my face in his neck. His clean scent and woodsy aftershave washed over me, and as always, any tension drained from my body while I was in his strong arms.

"I think you did great out there." I nipped at his ear, and his hands eased down my back to my ass that was barely covered with a pair of shorty-shorts. I squeaked when he gave a hard squeeze.

"That makes one of us."

I didn't like his reply at all, so I bit down harder on his lobe. "I'll reward you tonight."

He laughed, the sound rumbling from his chest and into mine. "I can't wait."

"Get a room!" Easton called from the bar.

Braden slid me slowly down his body, his erection pressing into my stomach. I turned around and planted my ass on his crotch.

"Jeez, Nik, that could kill a man." He grabbed my hips and started walking me through the crowd, each step rubbing my ass on his tented jeans.

Several teammates said hi, their voices barely audible above the din of chatter and the old rock song playing over the speakers. The team bar felt like home—the smell of beer, freshly showered men, and an unrestrained lust for life all crammed into a small space.

Braden's hard dick stayed wedged between my ass cheeks the entire way. By the time we made it to Easton and Kyrie, I was a giggling mess.

Easton gave Braden a grin. "Stop using Nikki as your boner garage. We have some celebrating to do." He looped an arm around Kyrie and kissed her, bending her back as if he wanted to devour her.

Braden sat on a bar stool and pulled me into his lap, his chest to my back. "You like teasing me, don't you?" His hands slid down my thighs, sending goosebumps rising along my skin.

"I don't know what you're talking—"

He squeezed a fistful of my hair and pulled me against him. When his lips hit my neck, I squirmed, his cock growing even harder beneath me. Growling against my skin, he sucked on my throat as his team milled around us, paying no mind to the two make-out sessions going on at the bar.

I jumped when Braden slid his hand up between my thighs. His fingers delved to my panties. I grabbed his bear paw and pushed it away, but not before his fingertips brushed the fabric over my pussy and sent fireworks skittering across my skin.

"Braden, not here." I fidgeted more, and he released me.

"Just wait until later. I'm going to turn your ass bright red for teasing me."

My pussy heated up another notch, and I wondered if he knew how wet he made me. I looked at him over my shoulder and batted my lashes. "Promise?"

He kissed me softly, his lips barely brushing against mine. But when he spoke, his voice was hard and low. "Count on it, baby."

"So, when is this dinner-with-the-parents thing supposed to happen?" Easton had come up for air as Kyrie poured our glasses full of beer.

"Saturday." I clapped like an idiot, but I couldn't stop the wave of excitement that rushed over me.

Braden stiffened beneath me, and not in the good way.

"What?" I turned so I sat across his lap, my right arm wrapped around his neck.

He shook his head. "Nothing. I'm just, just looking forward to it is all." He plastered a smile on his face. It was the fake, toothy smile I didn't like.

Easton snorted. "Yeah, you really look like you're raring to go."

"Shut up." Braden took a swig of his beer.

When he set his mug down, I put my hands on his cheeks and stared into his puppy-dog eyes. "My parents will love you. Dad loves all things baseball—"

"We know, *Nokona*." Kyrie snickered.

I sighed. As if I didn't get enough teasing about my name. My father had named me after a type of baseball glove. Love of the game was in my blood. My attraction to baseball players wasn't the least bit coincidental. I'd spent my youth watching my brother's high school baseball team—all those hot young guys in tight pants. It was no secret I was a cleat chaser through and through. But I'd never been caught up in a player until I'd met Braden.

"I think your dad has excellent taste in names." Braden smiled and clinked his mug to mine. We both drank, the usual foam coating my upper lip. I set my glass down and waited. But nothing happened. Braden kissed beer foam off my lips every chance he got, and he was so good at it. Those lips were a religious experience. But this time, he didn't.

I glanced to him and wiped the back of my hand across my mouth. He had a thousand-yard stare, his mouth drawn down at the corners. Worry tiptoed up my spine.

"Hey, baby." I ran the back of my hand down his cheek. "What's the matter?"

He came out of his daze and took another long swig. "I'm good. No worries. Um, so what am I supposed to call your parents?"

"My dad's name is John, and my mom's is Catherine, but she goes by Cat."

Easton spewed beer across the bar. "Kitty Cat?" He could barely get the words out, his whole body shaking as he laughed.

"What? No. Just Cat." I raised an eyebrow at Kyrie, but she was laughing into her hand, clearly in on the joke.

Easton locked eyes with Braden. "You motor-boating son-of-a-bitch!" He dissolved into peals of laughter as Kyrie shook her head and tried to hide her grin.

Braden shook beneath me. His lips were pinched together, and his eyes were about to pop out of his head from trying to contain his laughter.

"Oh my God, what is the joke, you idiots!" I stabbed a finger into Easton's chest.

"Have you never seen *Wedding Crashers*?" Easton wiped a tear and tried to settle down.

"No, why?"

"There's a character… Well there's a scene where …" Easton glanced at Braden again, who slowly shook his head. Taking the hint, Easton shrugged and grabbed his beer again. "It's, ah, it's not important." He put the glass to his lips and drank, and kept drinking as I glared at him.

"I'll tell you about it later." Kyrie patted my arm and tucked a lock of hair behind my ear. "*After* the dinner."

"Go ahead and tell me now—"

"No way." Braden finally spoke, the sound like a gunshot as he released his held breath.

"It's better this way." Kyrie smiled, mischief dancing in her eyes.

"Fine." I could wait until after, or I could just ask Professor Google when I got home. Either way, it didn't matter. The dinner would show my family that Braden was the perfect guy for me.

Braden finished his beer in record time and poured another. All four of us chatted and joked for the rest of the night. Braden and Easton even pranked the rookie by ordering him a pitcher of O'Doul's. The poor kid couldn't tell the difference.

Despite the fun, I caught Braden staring off far more than usual. Was it because of the dinner or something else? There was no point in asking. Braden wasn't known for opening up, not even with me sometimes. But the niggling worry in my stomach began to grow each time I noticed his mind was elsewhere. I resolved that the dinner would soothe all his concerns, because my parents would have no other option but to love him like I did. Problem solved.

Ives opened the door for us as we walked into my parents' home. Every time I came here, a sense of nostalgia washed over me. I'd grown up on the lush green lawns, playing on the wide front porch, and inside the large white house that sat atop a gentle rise. The green shutters looked exactly the same, and the wide front door gave the same slight creak it always did when it swung inward.

I hugged Ives, perhaps a little too hard.

He patted my back. "Good to see you again, too, Miss Nikki."

"Did you like Florida?"

He smiled, deep wrinkles around his mouth and eyes reminding me of his age. "I like it here at home better. But I think the air down there does something good for my joints."

"Spring in your step?"

He shook his bald head. "It doesn't do *that* much good, Miss Nikki."

Braden cleared his throat. I pulled him off the front porch and into the house. "Ives, this is my boyfriend, Braden Bradford."

Ives inclined his head slightly and studied Braden. "Nice

to meet you, young man. Come on in. Dinner is almost on the table."

Braden's hands couldn't stay still the entire way here. He would rub his nose, scratch along his thigh, drum on the steering wheel—do anything but relax. I took his damp palm in mine. He had nothing to worry about. In his light blue button-down shirt, open at the collar, and pressed khakis, he looked as handsome as ever.

I ran my hand down his smooth face and whispered, "Don't worry."

"You aren't, perchance, doing any hunting while you're here, are you?" Ives had laughter in his voice as he led us past the music room and my father's wood-paneled study. Baseball mementos lined the walls and shelves.

"No. Hope not." Braden pulled at his collar even though it wasn't touching his throat. I glanced down. I wore an A-line summer dress that cut mid-thigh, gathered at my waist, and hugged my bust. The top was sleeveless with a modest scoop, and the white material bore a large floral print. We looked like a perfect pair going to a picnic, or perhaps to watch a horse race. My parents would approve.

My white heels clicked on the polished wood floors as we passed the sun room, and Ives led us into the formal dining room.

I froze. Braden stopped at my side.

"Come in, come in!" Mom waved us toward the head of the table. A cacophony of "oh shits" played through my mind, but there was no turning back.

I forced a smile to my face, despite my burning need to strangle my mother.

"Nikki, you look amazing." Carter smiled his engaging smile. His blond hair was perfectly styled to fall in elegant waves, as if he'd just come in from a day at the beach.

My mother tittered as my father took a long pull on his glass of red. I walked to her slowly, almost mechanically. I glanced at Braden. He was sweating, and his gaze bounced from one person to the next, as if he didn't know who to speak to first.

I strode to my mother. "Mom."

She pulled me close and gave each of my cheeks an imaginary kiss. Her light gray hair didn't move even a centimeter, and she wore a white pant suit that she likely borrowed from Hilary Clinton's closet.

Dad wore seersucker pants, a pale gray polo, and a look of distaste as he gave Braden the once-over. My stomach churned, and I had to work to keep the smile on my face. Why was Carter here?

"Mom, Dad, this is my boyfriend, Braden Bradford."

"Mr. Graves." Braden shook my dad's hand. Then he hugged my mother, ass-out as was appropriate. She gave him the air-kiss treatment as well, but when she pulled back, her eyes narrowed.

"And I'm Carter." He held out his hand. "I've heard so much about you, Braden. Wonderful to finally meet you."

Braden shook his hand. "Thanks, I guess. Are you a brother I didn't know about or something?"

The acid in my stomach turned into a whirling tornado, and the tips of my ears went cold.

"No." There was Carter's too-perfect smile again. "I'm just an old friend of Nikki's." Before I could back away, he took me in his arms and gave me a long hug—definitely not ass-out, and definitely more than an 'old friend' would give.

I glared at Mom over Carter's shoulder. She gave a slight shrug and took a drink of wine. This was not going as expected. I'd been ambushed by none other than Carter Falkland, ex-boyfriend and heir to the largest paper products fortune in the world. Worse than that, it was obvious my mother had set it all up.

With more than a little effort, I pulled away from Carter's embrace and took Braden's hand. "This is my boyfriend."

"Yes, dear, you made that clear." Mom motioned to the table, each place setting arranged with a degree of precision that even a neuro-surgeon would envy. Three centerpieces of blue hydrangeas and yellow roses were placed at intervals along the table, though we only used five seats of the twenty-four.

Carter moved to pull a chair out for me, but Braden grabbed it first.

"Have a seat, babe." His assertive tone had me tingling in all the right places.

I smiled and said "thank you" before sitting. Braden sat to my right. Dad took the head of the table at my left, a frown firmly affixed to his face—thanks to Mother, I was sure. Mom and Carter moved to sit opposite us.

I glared at her as Carter pulled out her chair. She locked eyes with me, the challenge apparent. She'd been trying to get me back together with Carter for two years straight. She still hadn't given up, and now Braden was caught in a mother-daughter pissing match. I would win, but I had to be careful. Mom was craftier than a seventy-year-old at a scrapbooking convention.

She waved at the cook, who began serving the salad course. Braden kept wiping his palms down his pants, and a visible sweat mustache had formed along his upper lip. Dad scowled, Mom simpered, and Carter didn't take his light blue eyes off me. Tense was an understatement.

I cleared my throat. "Braden's the catcher for the Ravens. They won their game on Thurs—"

"Carter, how's the paper business going? I heard you're managing the finances." Mom began cutting her salad into very particular little squares, her silverware clicking against the plate.

"Oh, it's fine. I have to watch the market like a hawk, determine trends, use data to ensure I'm on top of everything. Just boring high-level mathematics, mostly calculus. Did you ever take a calculus class in college, Braden?" Carter smiled, a piece of lettuce in his teeth.

Braden paused mid-chew. "I didn't go to college."

Carter knew that, of course. I wanted to somehow kick him in the balls under the table.

"Oh, of course. Sorry." He sipped his lemon water, pinky

out. "I forgot that baseball players focus on physical exertions more than intellect."

"How much intellect does it take to waltz through college on Mommy and Daddy's money and then take a job at Daddy's shit-paper company?" I took an angry bite of salad, the Caesar dressing tart and tangy on my tongue.

Mom coughed into her hand and shot me a stony glare.

Braden patted my thigh. "It's all right, Nikki. We can't all be as physically fit as I am. Some people are better suited for sitting behind a desk all day, never getting their hands dirty, and playing on calculators. And then there are those of us who are better suited for more—" He glanced at me, the light in his eyes scandalous. "—physical exertions."

He slid his hand up my thigh, under my skirt, and ran his fingertips along my panties. I shuddered and fidgeted in my chair.

Carter took a larger gulp of lemon water and returned to his salad, eyes down.

"I saw your last game. Pity about that long ball. I thought it was gone." My father's frown had gone from full engagement to half-hearted. I had no doubt my mother had instructed him to be a disagreeable grump—which was quite natural to him, really—but his love of the game cut through her bullshit.

Mother, undeterred, tried again. "Carter, could you tell us—"

"I heard the guy that caught it is on the disabled list, though. Bruised his rib something terrible reaching out to get it." My father smiled at Braden. Mom was too late; the tide had turned to baseball.

"*Good*. Lucky son-of-a—" he glanced at my mother "—I mean, I thought I had him burned. But he got lucky."

My father and Braden fell into easy conversation over the ins and outs of the game as Carter and Mom sulked. I ate and drank contentedly, with Braden's hand between my thighs all the while.

CHAPTER SIX

BRADEN

AFTER DINNER, I WALKED up a giant spiral staircase behind Nik's dad and this Carter chump. I hadn't been able to get a good read on Mr. Graves, but I wasn't about to take any more shit off of Carter. Not a chance.

"Have you ever played *billiards*?" Carter popped his head back and glanced down at me with a shitty stare, like I was the help. It was the way guys like him seemed to look down at everyone.

"I know how to shoot pool. If that's what you're asking." I continued up the stairs that seemed to go on forever, and wished I was anywhere but there.

Carter belted out an obnoxious chuckle, the kind of shit that would be in a bad movie where the wealthy people laugh at the peasants. He'd taken any shot he could during dinner—doing his best to ding my intellect and puff himself up in front of Nikki and her parents. Her father managed to get in some baseball talk with me, but the rest of the time was taken up with Carter's stories. Nikki's mother practically drooled all over the smug bastard and gave me only sidelong glances. This wasn't my scene, and every comment from Carter reinforced that fact.

Calm down. It's just another hour or two and then you can make Nik scream your name and come on your dick.

I calmed at my thoughts and smiled up at Carter, knowing I'd be balls-deep in the pussy he was after. I'd already won.

When we reached the top, my head was on a swivel, taking in the scenery. Ornate woodwork and shelves stretched around the expansive walls, and the carpet was a rich cream color. Fancy leather furniture and chairs surrounded three sides of the pool table, which sat in the middle of the room. A full bar and large flat-screen television rounded out the place. It was the most hoity-toity fucking man cave in history, and I couldn't help but snicker.

"Something funny, Braden?" Carter leaned against the back of the closest chair.

I didn't respond, just stared him down.

Mr. Graves acted oblivious to the rising tension as we followed him toward the table. "Billiards is a fine combination of art and science, Braden."

Somebody blow my brains out.

Whipping his goldilocks around, Carter glanced back once more and smirked.

"Much like baseball," Mr. Graves continued. He turned to us when we reached a selection of fancy pool cues hanging on a wooden rack alongside the television. "It requires patience, focus, strategy, and muscle memory."

Rich people always baffled me. It was funny, because technically I was one of them now, but I was anything but comfortable in this mansion. Baseball came naturally to me. Shooting pool was trying to put the ball in the hole. What was this guy on about?

"I watch the way you play the game. You're a very intelligent ballplayer." He smiled and turned back to select a stick.

"Hear that, Carter? I'm intelligent." My words were muttered under my breath.

Carter caught them and turned to me.

"What, pretty boy? Don't like the competition?" I pretend-kissed the air at him and waggled my eyebrows. Fuck it. I was going to have some fun with this prick instead of stewing on all the bullshit running through my brain.

He raised his chin so that he could sneer at me once

more. I'm sure he thought it was cool, but it made him look like an ass clown.

"You're an imbecile who cashed in on the lottery. Because you're good at a game. That's not competition for me." He flashed that cocky smirk at me again.

Prick.

"All right boys, choose your weapons." Mr. Graves, still ignoring our sparring, had finally selected his pool cue.

"Gladly." I grabbed the first one I saw, whipped around, and pretended to take a swing at Carter, stopping the stick inches from his rib cage. He flinched like a quivering cunt bag. I couldn't verify, but I'm certain he pissed his frilly panties a little.

"Jesus! Just messing with you, Carter. Lighten up. He said weapons, so I thought maybe we were going to fight with these things."

Mr. Graves stared at me, finally catching on to the strain in the air. "What are you doing?"

Something about the way he said it, the way Carter was smirking—heat rushed into my face, and I gripped the cue as hard as I could. "Nothing. Won't happen again." My words came through my teeth.

Carter shook his head. "Embarrassing. You'd think you could hand an idiot a stick in the twenty-first century and they wouldn't go all primitive. Turns out you can't." He shrugged and whipped his head back around with a shit-eating grin.

"Let's have a drink. Maybe that will help us warm up for the *friendly* game." Mr. Graves walked to the fully stocked bar and set down three high ball glasses. Carter and I followed him over and watched as he poured.

"This brings back memories." Carter tapped his fingers on the bar. "I haven't had your good whiskey since that time Nikki and I snuck in here while you and Cat were sleeping."

I shifted from one foot to the next, ready to whip this guy's ass for just mentioning Nikki. Then again, curiosity began to overwhelm me. How well did he know her?

"Oh?" Mr. Graves tsked. "Stealing the good stuff? When was that? I don't remember."

"It's been a few years. You and Cat had just returned from a long weekend away." Carter took his glass and sipped, his eyes locked on mine. "I'd stayed to keep Nikki company *all* weekend. We had a great time."

That was enough for me.

"How about I break this stick off in your ass, Carter McShitPaper?"

Mr. Graves spewed high-dollar whiskey all over the bar, and started to choke on it. Carter stiffened straight as a goddamn board, as I stepped toward him. He tugged at his five-hundred-dollar shirt collar.

Mr. Graves darted forward and somehow wedged his lanky frame between us. Carter smirked at me once more. That was all it took. I blew my lid.

"Don't think I won't go through him and pound your goddamn pretty-boy face!" My voice boomed through the house, echoing off the fancy walls and other expensive shit these people cared about.

"I think it's time you leave." Mr. Graves words were slow and steady, but his fingers on my arm were trembling.

"Happy to. And I apologize, to *you*. But not to the fancy-feast bowtie-pussy behind you. He says another word about my girl, and I'll pound his ass!"

Two sets of heels clacked against the stairs like twin jackhammers. Nikki appeared and came scurrying in our direction with her mother hot on her trail. "Whose ass are you about to pound?" She stopped about two feet away and folded her arms over her chest.

Shit.

My skin burned hot from head to toe, and rage coursed through my veins. The longer I stood enclosed within these walls, with these people, the worse I felt. I'd never been this way in my entire life. But something about Nikki and that cunt face Carter boiled everything to the surface. I attempted to steady my breathing. It wasn't happening. Even so, I stepped away from Nikki's father and headed toward the door.

"I know whose ass I used to pound." Carter flashed a smile at Nik.

The Hulk returned. I flipped back around and shot Carter the bird. "Fuck you, Nick Carter! You goddamn backdoor boy! Your teeth are about to end up on this carpet!"

"Let's go, Braden." Nik dug her nails into my forearm, and I stared at her bright-pink face. I couldn't tell if it was anger, embarrassment, sadness—I hoped it was none, but knew it was probably all three.

I dropped my gaze to the floor. My rage sparred with the worry I'd embarrassed Nikki. Or worse, hurt her. *Fuck.* "Okay," I nodded, "Let's go."

I strode to the stairs with Nik at my side. She was still gripping my arm.

"I'm sorry, everyone." I didn't bother turning to look at them. They didn't give a fuck about my apology.

"Yeah, you should be." Carter's voice echoed around us, but I was done with him. Fuck it.

Nik dropped my arm and flipped around. "You need to shut your goddamn mouth, Carter! You shouldn't even be here! Braden is my boyfriend, not you. I don't care what sort of game you and Mom are playing. You and I are *never* going to get back together." She stomped her foot. "So stop trying to make fetch happen!"

I glanced back and the three of them stood silent while Nik shook a finger at them. It was pretty goddamn hot to be honest. I hadn't seen her so angry since Easton beat the shit out of Kyrie's ex in the bar.

Nikki's mother put her hands on her bony hips. "Just wait a—"

Nik shook, anger radiating from her small frame. "No! You wait a minute. Like nobody knows what the hell you did tonight. This isn't all on Braden. You know exactly what you did, and this night is done. I wish I'd never brought him here. You're an embarrassment." Nik twirled around and blew past me. "Come on. *Now.*"

I chased after her down the stairs. My dick tried to rocket through my zipper at the sight of her storming off, but I had a feeling she was about to deflate the fuck out of the poor guy. She lit into me before we could make it out the door.

"What the fuck, Braden?" She yanked the front door open and stormed down the porch steps toward the car. "I don't know what your deal is."

When she turned to face me halfway down the circle drive, the moonlight reflected the tears suspended in the corner of her eyes. "Where are you? I know you're in there. I miss you."

I could tell she was about to lose it. My heart raced, and worry pooled in the pit of my stomach. I stared at the ground and kicked at a crack in the driveway. "I'm fine."

"You're not fine." She folded her arms and scowled.

I looked back at the trio of assholes now standing on the porch. The sight of Carter had my blood heating to an alarming degree. I ground my teeth together. "Not here."

"I need to know, *now.* You're not getting me in that car until I know what the problem is. You haven't been yourself since the game the other night."

"I said not now." I stomped past her as tears streamed down her cheeks.

She didn't follow me. I glanced back, and she covered her mouth with her palm.

I froze stiff. She stood there, hurting right in front of me. I wanted to hug her and tell her everything, but all I could see was Carter up there smirking his fucking dick off. Her mother tried to hide a smile when I looked at her, and failed miserably.

Everything from the past few days rushed out of me, and Nik was the one in my sights, waiting to take the brunt of it. My feet pounded on the pavement, and I leaned down to her face. "My stats have been shit all year. Nothing is going my goddamn way. Coach called me into his office after the game. Know what he said? *Do you, Nik?*"

I kept my voice low as she sobbed into her hand. "They're looking to trade me, or just cut me loose. That play that made all the highlight reels might be the last bit of baseball that I have to hold onto. Me. Failing. What the fuck am I if I'm not on a ballfield?" My voice rose. "Shit! Shit is all I am. Your boyfriend Carter up there got that one right. Didn't he?"

She continued to weep in front of me, and I still couldn't stop the onslaught.

"I-I didn't know that, B-Braden. Y-you didn't tell me."

I clenched my fists. "Maybe because all you could talk about was meeting your parents." I held my hands up and mocked her. "Oh, what a great idea that was! Look at them. Hey, they're happy now." I walked back to the car.

She stilled.

"Baseball is all I've got. And all you cared about was this stupid night." I hated myself as soon as the words left my mouth.

"B-baseball is all y-you've got?" She barely got the words out before the sobs increased tenfold.

Reality crashed into me like a Mack truck. Carter wasn't the biggest prick here. It was me. *What the fuck did I just do?* I looked away and took in a huge breath of night air. "I'm sorry. I just—you know what I mean. Come home. We'll figure it out."

Mr. Graves walked down the steps and put his arm around Nik's shoulders.

I took a step toward her. "Nikki, please?"

She was damn near catatonic, just standing there, staring at the ground as her tears splattered on the concrete. I'd reduced her to this, all because I couldn't handle my own bullshit. She buried her face in her father's shoulder and sobbed.

Regret ripped through my chest, the pain sudden and searing. "Nik, please? I'm sorry."

Mr. Graves looked up at me. "Maybe you should head home, Braden. You two can sort this out tomorrow."

I couldn't look away from her. "Is that what you want?"

Carter piped up. "Of course it's what she—"

Mr. Graves turned to Carter and held up a hand. "Zip it, son."

Nikki still refused to look at me, and my heart tightened like a vise was clamping down on it with every second that passed. Mr. Graves turned around slowly. "My daughter has had enough tonight, Braden. Just give her a little time."

I shook my head again, grinding my jaw and staring at that smirking motherfucker. But I knew Mr. Graves was right. Something about the way he spoke to Carter—I knew Nik would be safe. But he wasn't the threat. I was. I'd done a lot of damage in a short amount of time. *Fuck.*

My eyes started to mist, and I didn't want Carter to have the satisfaction of seeing me cry for the first time in fifteen years. I nodded. "O-okay then." I glanced at Nik one last time, and wanted the whole ordeal to be a nightmare I'd wake up from in a cold sweat, with her next to me to grab hold of. She still trembled against her father. "Sorry for ruining your evening."

I walked to the car, regret ripping through my body with every step. When I pulled out of the driveway, and Nik disappeared in the rearview mirror, I couldn't keep the tears at bay anymore. What had I just done?

CHAPTER SEVEN

NIKKI

KYRIE PULLED ME INTO her arms as Easton closed the front door of their apartment behind us. I still hadn't been able to stop crying. Dad had dropped me here so I could stay the night with Kyrie. I couldn't stand to be anywhere near Carter or Mom after everything that had happened.

Kyrie shushed me and ran her hand through my hair. "It'll be okay. Just tell me what happened."

"I'll just be, uh, I'll be doing the dishes or something." Easton took off toward the kitchen like the hounds of hell were after him.

"Fat chance," Kyrie mumbled and guided me toward their bedroom. She set me on the edge of the bed and wiped her thumbs across my cheeks. "I'll get you some water. Hang on."

My phone beeped again and again. I dug it out of my bag and turned the ringer off. Braden would have to wait. I couldn't speak to him, couldn't even think about him without feeling a knife in my ribs.

"I don't want water." I swiped at my eyes.

Kyrie kept walking toward their bathroom, her yoga pants clinging to her round ass. "That was really a cover. I'm getting you a makeup remover wipe. You look like a sad raccoon."

I cried harder. First, at the thought of looking ugly, and second, at the realization I'd never have an ass as nice as Kyrie's.

55

She disappeared into the bathroom and, before long, reappeared with a wet wipe, a box of tissues, and a small tumbler of water. "Let me get you cleaned up a bit."

I let her wipe my face. "Am I ugly?" I asked through my haze of self-pity. My sobs had quieted, but I couldn't stop my tears.

"Are you kidding?" She laughed and gently scrubbed beneath my eyes. "I've wished for your looks a million times."

That cheered me a little. Jealousy always made me feel like I was doing something right. After Kyrie finished cleaning me up, I blew my nose and took a few sips of water. She crawled to the head of the bed and lay down. Her perfect, large tits taunted me beneath her snug tank top. *Showoff.* Patting the mattress next to her, she said, "Come on, give me all the dirty details."

I obliged, flopping down next to her and burying my face in her pillow. "Braden lost his mind in front of my parents and made me feel like shit."

"Braden's mind feels your tits? Is that what you said?" She smoothed a hand up and down my back.

I rolled to the side and stared up at her. "No, he went nuts because Carter was at the dinner."

Kyrie knew all the details of my past, so Carter was nothing new.

Kyrie whistled. "Does he know about you and Carter?"

"He does now." I sighed. "And he yelled at me in front of everyone about how baseball is his life." The ache he'd set off in my chest came back with full force. "And that it's the only thing he cares about." A sob rocketed up from my lungs.

Kyrie pulled me to her and held me. We laid side by side for a few minutes until my crying fit subsided enough for her to speak.

"He loves you. Something must have set him off. Something bad. I'm not making excuses for him." The hand she was using to pet my hair clutched the strands a little too tightly.

"Ow."

"Sorry." She resumed her stroking. "I just don't like the thought of him yelling at you."

"He wasn't himself. Not at all. And it wasn't just because of Carter. He said Coach pulled him into his office a few days ago." I dropped my voice to a whisper. "He may be traded."

"Oh, shit." Her eyes widened.

"Yeah, he didn't tell me, not until tonight. He should have told me." I couldn't have done anything, but at least we could have carried the burden together. "He didn't trust me enough to tell me. It hurts." I buried my face in her ample tits. They were soft and warm, just like I remembered. Easton really was a lucky man.

"I don't think it was a trust issue. Braden is the sort of guy who wants to make everyone else happy. He's always smiling, cutting up, having a good time, and most of all, making sure everyone around him is having a great time. He probably didn't want to bring you down."

"That doesn't make it okay." I snuggled closer to her chest pillows.

"Of course not. I'd like to smack the shit out of him." She sighed. "But I think the pressure of meeting your parents, plus having to deal with Carter, *on top* of the trade talks… Maybe it was all too much for him. Not an excuse, just an explanation."

"Does Easton sleep like this every night, right here in the sweet spot?"

She laughed, her tits jiggling in a friendly sort of way. "Easton would say that I have an even sweeter spot he'd like to be in all night long."

I laughed a little. "That's why I like him. He has his priorities straight."

"Did Braden say where they might trade him to?"

"No, he said that Coach—"

"Trade?" Easton leaned against the doorframe. "I hate to

interrupt your 'Terms of Endearment' moment, but you can't say the word trade around here and expect me to sit back and ignore it. What's going on?"

I recounted how Braden had acted, including the bombshell about a possible trade.

Easton went from pissed to shocked and back to pissed. "That fucker didn't even say a word to me about it." He flexed his fists and paced around the room. "I'm going to ring his goddamn bell."

"Easton, calm down." Kyrie shifted, leaving me without my delightful tit perch. "Nikki needs our help, not for you to go caveman like Braden."

I sat up and rubbed my eyes. "He said it was just 'talks' not an actual trade, so he can still stay with the Ravens, right?"

Easton shook his head and continued his pacing, his big body making the lamps rattle with each angry step. "If they start shit like that, they usually finish it. They don't talk about trades unless there's a real chance it could happen. Fuck!" He slapped his hand down on the dresser. "I'm going to kick his sorry ass!"

"Easton." Kyrie stood and walked to him. She pried his arms apart and wrapped them around her. "This isn't about you, baby. It's about Nikki and Braden. Can you calm down enough to help her figure out what to do?" She stared up at him with her green eyes.

Easton melted for her, turning back into the teddy bear I'd come to know and love.

He sighed and rubbed her back before glancing over to me. "I'll help. Of course I'll help."

Our apartment was dark when I walked in. I shut the door behind me and navigated through the living room from memory. A hall light showed me to our bedroom. When I opened the door, Braden's gentle snore greeted me. Beer bottles covered his nightstand, and he lay on his back, his forearm thrown across his eyes. Tissues littered the floor next to the bed.

I wasn't surprised. He'd sent me over fifty "I'm sorry" voice mails and texts, each one drunker than the last. I stared at him, his dress shirt wrinkled and his hair in an untidy mess. Even after what he'd done at my parents' house, I loved him. Something told me I always would.

On my side of the bed, he'd arranged three pillows next to him in a line, as if a person were lying there. As if *I* were there.

I dropped my bag on the dresser, and he roused a bit. He turned to the pillow-Nikki and hugged her to his chest. My bruised heart warmed at the sight.

When he murmured "Nik," fresh tears welled in my eyes. He was a grown man, but handled problems like a teenage boy—bottling them up until he exploded. We would work through it together. And I would do everything I could to help him through the trade issue. But right then, all I wanted was him.

I walked to the bed, unzipping my dress as I went. It hit the floor and I stepped out of it. Peeling my panties down my legs, I kicked them away. Then I unclasped my bra and tossed it.

"Braden." I climbed on top of him, straddling his hips.

His dark eyelashes fluttered until he was awake, staring up at me.

"Nik, I'm sorry." The moonlight glinted off the pools of sadness forming in his eyes.

"It's okay." I unbuttoned his shirt. "Just don't let it happen again."

"I should never have said those things. I didn't mean them—"

"I know. You should have told me about the trade."

"You're right. I thought I could, I don't know, handle it

somehow. Wh-what are you doing?" He ran his hands up my thighs and his cock thickened beneath my pussy.

"That worked out well, didn't it? Got it all handled, did you?" I dragged my nails down his chest.

The teary glint left his eye and was replaced with heat. "Are you punishing me?"

I pinched his nipples. "Do you want to be punished? You certainly deserve it."

He let his eyes rove my body, lingering on my tits and then on my pussy. I unbuttoned and unzipped his pants. When I yanked down his boxers, his cock sprang free. I gripped it, stroking slowly with one hand as I rubbed my pussy back and forth over the base.

"I don't like being punished." He groaned as I bore down on him, letting him feel how wet I was. "But I'd like to apologize by fucking you until you can't walk straight."

In one smooth movement, he'd rolled on top of me. The line of pillows were beneath me, pushing me closer to Braden. He shucked his shirt, pants, and shorts off, then pressed his chest against mine.

"I'm sorry." He kissed my cheek. "I'm sorry." He kissed my neck. Again and again he told me how sorry he was as he dotted me with sweet kisses. He took my hard nipple in his mouth and bit down. I moaned and dug my nails into his side.

He grunted and rocked his hips against me, rubbing his slick cock head up and down the length of my pussy. "I need you."

His tongue traced a line of heat from my nipple to my mouth, and when he kissed me, he took more than just my breath. I forgave him, but more than that, I loved him more than I'd ever loved anything. He slanted his head, his tongue plunging against mine. My skin warmed, and my pussy tightened with anticipation.

He kept teasing me, rubbing the head of his cock back and forth over my clit until I was writhing beneath him. I wanted to tell him how much I loved him, but his insistent kiss took any speech from my lips. He snagged both my wrists and pinned them next to me. My heart raced, thrumming against his hard chest as he positioned his cock at my entrance.

Breaking the kiss, he moved to my neck, sucking my skin between his teeth. I moaned, and he gripped my wrists harder. The little sting of pain poured more fuel on the fire, and I needed him inside me like I needed my next breath.

"Please," I whimpered as he ran his teeth across my throat.

His hips jerked, but he maintained control. "Beg me."

"Please, please, please Braden!" I tried to scoot down to get him inside me, but he moved his hips back.

"Tell me exactly what you want." He pinned me with his dark eyes. "Beg."

My pussy was on fire. I had to give in. It was the only way to get what I needed. "You. I want you. I want you to fuck me hard. Your cock deep inside me. I want your come. I want you to come inside me."

"Jesus, Nik." His voice was gravelly, dripping with sex.

"Please," I whispered.

He bit down on my shoulder and plunged inside me. I squealed at the intrusion, the slight sting, and then the wave of pleasure. I dug my heels into the backs of his thighs as he pulled out to his tip and shoved deep inside me again.

"Braden." I tried to reach up and touch him, but he didn't release my wrists. I was caught.

He pulled out again and started fucking me hard, the sound of his skin slapping on mine echoing around the room. Each impact made my tits shake and my pussy hungry for more. Every hard thrust amped up the tension in my clit.

I spread my legs wider, putting my heels in the air. He kept up his powerful thrusts, grunting with each effort and latching his mouth to my neck. His hard strokes hit me just right, my spot and my clit already buzzing closer to the edge.

I wanted to hold out and come with him. But, then he did the one thing that makes waiting impossible.

"You like being my little slut?" His mouth was at my ear.

I moaned and spread my legs even wider.

"Answer me, Nikki. Are you my little slut?" He thrusted harder, punctuating his words.

"Yes."

"Are you going to come on my cock like a good little slut?"

"Oh my God." I couldn't breathe. I couldn't think when he talked to me like that.

"I can already tell your greedy cunt wants to come." He licked the shell of my ear.

My pussy constricted even tighter, and I closed my eyes as the wave crested.

"Tell me you're my slut, and I'll let you come." He pounded me in hard, steady strokes.

"I-I'm your slut." When the words left my mouth, my hips froze.

"That's it, little slut. Come on my cock." He bit my neck right below my ear, and I came on a scream. My legs trembled as he kept fucking me all the way through my orgasm, each impact another spark in the explosion of pleasure he'd set off inside me.

"So goddamn tight, Nik. Your pussy's trying to get me to come, but I won't. Not until my little slut has had her second."

His words were lost in a jumble of endorphins, everything tumbling around inside me as my body shattered under the weight of him and his filthy words. By the time I came back down, the neighbors knew who lived in this apartment.

Releasing my wrists, he ran a hand down to my breast. He squeezed the small mound, then pinched my stiff peak. "You almost got me. Those sounds you make. Fuck." He bent his head to my other nipple and sucked it into his mouth.

I arched my back and ran my hands through his hair. "You make me make them."

He maintained a languid pace, his cock touching every part of my pussy. "I know. You're about to make some more."

He rose onto his knees and roughly pushed me over onto my stomach.

"Hey!"

Before I could make a half-hearted protest, he settled onto my back, his sweat-slicked chest pressing me into the mattress. His cock wedged between my ass cheeks as he straddled my legs. I struggled beneath him, but he kept thrusting.

"You aren't getting away, slut. Still mine."

I moaned and buried my face in the pillow as he sucked on the back of my neck. One of his hands yanked my hair and the other trailed down my side, sending shivers through me. He raised up slightly. Then I felt his stiff head pressing into me again.

He surged forward. With my legs together, the sensation of being filled was almost too intense.

"Goddammit, so tight." He dropped a kiss between my shoulder blades and braced himself with one hand on the bed. The other gripped my hip and lifted my ass. "Fuck yes." He started pounding me, rubbing my spot and sending the flames inside me spiraling higher.

I stretched my arms out and braced against the headboard. His pounding hips shook the nightstands, the bed, everything in the room, and I found myself lifting my hips even higher, wanting every bit of contact.

"That's it. Give me all of that pussy, my little slut."

My nipples tightened into hyper sensitive tips as they rubbed against the sheets. I turned my head to the side as Braden put one large hand on my upper back, pushing me down into the bed. He slid the other one beneath me and began strumming my clit. I kicked my feet at the wave of need that shot through me. He didn't stop, just kept fucking me, pressing me beneath him, and fingering my most sensitive spot.

I rocked my hips back to him stroke for stroke, and his groans grew lower, his grunts more pronounced.

"I'm going to coat my little slut's pussy." He slammed hard and slow, our bodies crashing together as my hips began to seize. "Is that what you want?"

"Yes," I breathed.

"Come on my cock, slut. Come, and tell me who you want to blow inside your tight cunt."

"You." I squeaked as my pussy clamped down on him. "You, Braden, please, Braden…" The rest of my words were lost in a low moan as my orgasm rushed over me like a crashing wave.

"Fuck!" Braden pumped inside, his cock stiffening even more. Then he gripped my ass hard enough to leave a mark and thrust deep as my pussy milked every last drop from him. "Jesus Titty-Fucking Christ, Nik." He leaned over my back and pulled my sweaty hair away from my neck. "We should have recorded that."

I tried to nod, but my muscles didn't obey. "I agree," I panted. "We could show it to our kids every Christmas and Fourth of July."

He laughed and kissed my shoulder. "Fuckers would be lucky to get a treat like that twice a year."

I craned my head back, and he claimed my mouth with one of his signature kisses.

When he finally leaned away and pulled out, he smirked down at me. "Thanks for my punishment."

CHAPTER EIGHT

BRADEN

"I CAN'T BELIEVE YOU didn't fucking tell me." Easton fumbled through his locker, knocking shit around like a big oaf.

"What do you want me to say? I just figured I needed to step up my game." I strapped the elastic from one of my shin guards across my calf and hooked the metal together.

"We're supposed to be boys. You should've told me. That shit ain't cool."

"Hey, E?" I tilted my head up to the big fucker with as serious a face as I could muster.

"Yeah, what's up?"

"I fucked Kasey last night." I maintained my composure as he leered in my direction. "It's true. Every word. Turned her straight. She loves the D now." It became harder not to burst into laughter, but I had to keep a straight face. For the good of the land.

"I'm being serious." He ripped his jacket out of the locker and tucked it up under his arm.

"I'm dead serious. It was a little weird at first, because I kept seeing your face when I would look at her. But I just closed my eyes and went with it."

His big heavy cleat nearly ripped the carpet from the floor as he spun to walk away.

"Aww, come on, man. If we can't joke about me fucking your gay sister then what do we have left? *Nothing.* That's what. It's like a goddamn convent in here." I slapped the other shin guard against my leg and began strapping it up.

Easton turned back around, apparently still pissed. "This is serious. You know they don't fuck around once the 't word' starts getting tossed around. And what about Nik? I should beat your ass for that. She's devastated. And I don't give a shit how many times you called her your slut last night. It doesn't make it all better." He cracked a slight grin at his final two sentences.

I held my fist out. "Give it up."

"Respect." He tapped my knuckles and we both grinned.

"I'm being for real about the other stuff though. You have to talk to me. We can figure this out, together." His hands went to his hips like an angry wife as he scolded me.

Ramirez walked around the corner just in time to catch the end of our conversation and see Easton standing there like a desperate housewife. He stopped dead in his tracks and held both his hands up.

Easton whipped his head around and shot him a glare. "What? A couple guys can't talk out a compromise in the locker room? This is conflict resolution 101. It says so in this book I've been read—" He froze and squeezed his eyes shut.

Ramirez and I both glanced to each other and shook our heads back and forth. Then we both eyed the gigantic woman standing between us.

"Reading what?" I smirked.

Easton's face turned pinker than Nik's pussy. "Fuck you guys."

Ramirez scratched his chin. "Hey E, speaking of that, I've been meaning to ask you a question."

I waited for the punchline. Ramirez was a jokester like us, and his shit was usually gold.

"What's that?" Easton sighed and scrubbed a hand over his face.

"Do you ever use that subscribe feature on Amazon?" Ramirez's face was stone cold. He nearly made me a believer.

Easton wrinkled his nose and leaned in as though he didn't hear the question. "Umm, no. Why?"

"You can save like five dollars a month on your tampons if you subscribe. I'm being for real right now. My girl does that shit. It gets me like two extra beers a month at happy hour. You should look into it." His deadpan delivery had me on the brink of a full-blown seizure while I tried not to laugh.

Easton balled his hands into fists and I noticed a vein bulging from his neck. Ramirez held his hands up once more as a peace offering. He walked over toward Easton as if it were an Aaron Sorkin style monologue.

"You think I'm teasing you, but I'm not." He stopped in front of Easton and began showing signs that he might break character, twitching slightly, but somehow he maintained. His head tilted up to meet Easton's eyes as Easton's chest started to rise and fall in heavy waves. "They'll deliver that shit right to the clubhouse if you put the address in." Ramirez glanced over at me and flipped two fingers up at me. "In two days if you got *Prime* shipping." He turned back to Easton. "Extra heavy flow tampons in two days, man. You believe that?"

I was nearly dead on the floor. Ramirez's Oscar-worthy performances during his jokes were legend.

He reached up and pretended to brush some dust off of Easton's shoulders. "Anyway. Just thought you should know. Spreading the love and what not. You two gentlemen have yourselves a wonderful afternoon." He tipped his cap to Easton and started to walk away.

Easton turned to me with the set of crazy eyes he used when he was about to start up some shenanigans. I laughed, clutching my side as he motioned toward Ramirez's back. I stood and pointed to my shin guards, alerting Easton they'd make noise if I moved too suddenly.

He gave me a thumbs up and a huge grin spread across his face. "Ramirez?"

"Yes, sir!" Ramirez came walking back over.

Easton reached back and put his fist on the back of his thigh where Ramirez couldn't see, and held one finger down.

"Tell me more about this prime shipping. I don't get on Amazon much."

Ramirez looked at me like the giant was a strange alien. "He umm, he knows I was making fun of him, right? I can't ever tell with this one here."

Easton put a second finger down. Three meant it was time to unleash hell. "Do they have like, all kinds of stuff on Amazon? Like anything you could want?"

Ramirez gave in, seemingly convinced E hadn't caught on to his tomfoolery. "Yeah man, anything you want is on there. Seriously."

Easton's hand on his leg started to tremble. It was almost go time. "What about say...*Chinese finger traps!*" He shot the third finger down and snagged Ramirez by the waist. He whipped the smaller man around and held him from behind.

Easton dry humped him from the back, and I grabbed the top of his head and started hip thrusting at his face.

"Goddamn, he's tight as fuck. Switch-a-roo?" Easton laughed, unable to fight it any longer.

I nodded and we both started to shout. "Switch that ass from front to back, slap that ass and fuck the crack!"

We flipped him around as he tried to swing at us. E took the mouth and I took the ass. Ramirez squirmed, and tried to get away. After E and I had our fill, we finally let him break free from our assault.

He swiped his hat from his head and pointed back and forth at both of us, obviously faking his anger. "Y'all motherfuckers ain't right. You need Jesus." He stormed away, mumbling. "Can't nobody ever be serious in this place." He faced us from the doorway. "This is a place of business, gentlemen. A commercial enterprise. It's to be *respected!*" He scoffed and disappeared into the tunnel that led out to the field.

"Did you at least get to finish?" I plopped back down onto the bench.

"Yeah, he's a swallower, so no evidence." Easton's big melon of a head rotated toward me, and we both doubled over.

"That guy is fucking insane." Easton sat down on the bench next to me as I pulled my chest protector over my head.

"Yup. Fucking hilarious. Fits right in."

"That's what she said."

"Nice. What was that all about anyway?" I sat down on the stool in front of my locker, facing Easton.

"Just some hazing." Easton's eyes darted away from me, toward the other side of the locker room.

"Cut the shit. All that compromise bullshit. Relationship stuff. You been doing some reading?" I cocked my head sideways and stared at him.

His face went pale. "Please don't make me tell you." He paused for a second and shrugged. "Yeah, you're gonna make me tell you." He let out a long sigh. "I've been reading some relationship books."

I tried to hold back a laugh, but I'm certain he could see it building in my cheeks.

"Fuck it. Never mind." He shot to his feet.

"Nah man. I'll be cool. I swear. You can tell me. Sit back down."

He lowered back to the bench, but with caution. "I'm thinking—" He drew out the last word. "—about, well, you know?"

"No, actually I have no clue what you are saying right now." I truly didn't.

"About proposing. And I've been trying to work on conflict resolution. I want to be the best man I can be for Kyrie, and I know I have kind of a temper. So I've been reading books and stuff on it. Also, to umm—"

"Go on." I mashed my lips together to keep from erupting in laughter. It wasn't the fact that he was doing this. It was a good thing. But, there was just something funny about how uncomfortable it made him, and the fact he was the size of a really cut Andre the Giant.

"Work on some of my blow ups. When I get mad." He

dropped his face into his palms, but then quickly turned his head back up at me. "Which reminds me. This conversation isn't about me and my temper. It's about you and your dip-shittery. Why the fuck didn't you tell me about the trade talk with Coach? And why the fuck did you blow up on Nik? They had to keep me from driving to your house and beating your ass in the middle of the night."

Regret ripped through my bones and landed in my stomach. "I don't know, okay. I didn't want to worry people. All I have to do is—"

"Tell the people who care about you. So they can help you shoulder some of this shit. You can't carry it all around. And you love Nik. Why the fuck would you tell her that all you care about is baseball? Do you know what that did to her? She jokes and brushes things off, but it destroyed her."

Fuck me. I hadn't thought about the way she might've interpreted that. Even when she asked me the question in the driveway it didn't fully sink in. I was caught up in my own head—my own bullshit. "I didn't mean it like that. You know what I'm saying? Right? Like, this has been the dream since we were kids. We worked our whole lives for it. I guess I just assumed, I don't know, that it was compartmentalized from everything else, if that makes sense? Of course Nik is a huge part of my life. I love her."

"Well, like I said. You can use your 'sit on my dick' tricks, but that doesn't mean she'll forgive and forget, even if she says that. Women are funny that way. They say 'oh yeah, everything is great'. But it isn't. They don't forget anything. *Ever.* And don't think you don't owe me. Your girlfriend hogged Kyrie's tits all night."

"I do apologize, as that is a mortal sin. A tit-free evening is no bueno, at all. But seriously, what the fuck am I supposed to do?" I rose. It was almost game time. I'd gone the past few days thinking Nik and I were good. Apparently, I thought wrong.

"I don't know, man. You need to talk to a chick. Buying Kyrie a Kindle was like, the extent of my creativity. I'd usually say flowers and chocolate. But that is only good for one fuck up. I'm assuming you've already used up that freebie?"

"I have. I sure have done that. Yes."

"As have I. Naturally. But, figure it out. And when it comes to the trade thing, you need to tell me that shit up front next time. Don't be a hero. You ain't motherfucking Captain America. His dick is way bigger than yours, and much smaller than mine."

I snorted. "Deal."

"Alright then. Play the way you always do. Numbers will pick up. You're the heart of the team. Everyone knows it. Nobody works harder than you. The front office will see that. Nut the fuck up."

"I already did. In Ramirez's ass." I laughed.

Easton chuckled. "Yeah you did."

CHAPTER NINE

NIKKI

I TYPED THE LAST few lines of my article on the terrors of too-hot wax or the lurking danger of ingrown hairs. All in all, I felt it was a solid piece for the beauty section. And I couldn't help but smile at the thought of my name being tagged at the end.

After emailing it over to Kyrie, I left my office and practically pranced over to hers. "Did you get it?"

She looked up from her typing, her reading glasses balanced near the tip of her nose. "What?"

"I sent you my wax story."

"When?" She went back to her work, her fingers flying across the keys.

"I don't know. Like, thirty seconds ago." I plopped down onto her small love seat and stared at her city view. One day I'd have a window office and make my (attractive male) secretary get me coffee and be my little bitch.

Her email pinged, and she smirked at me. "I got it."

I leaned forward, anticipation sending my left foot into a tapping frenzy. "Are you going to read it?"

She glanced at me. "Right now?"

"Yes right now!"

She laughed and shook her head. "Calm down. I'll give it a look. Hang on." A few more clicks and her eyes flew back and forth across the screen.

"Well?" I leaned far enough forward that there was a pretty good chance I might topple over onto the floor.

"Shh." Her eyes kept going back and forth like they were eating a corn cob. The corn cob of pussy pouf maintenance.

Once finished, she leaned back and gave me a grin. "Needs a copy edit. Otherwise, I think it's going to work perfectly."

I clapped and squeed. "Really?"

"Yes, really. You kept it toned down just like Graciela asked. Good work."

I jumped up and ran around her desk to squeeze her.

"Can't breathe." She said after several moments of me pressing her face to my chest.

"Sorry. I'm just so—oh my God, so excited!"

"I can see that, and you should be. Your own byline in *Style and Substance*. Things are looking up. Soon, all this—" she waved a hand at the messy pile of papers on her desk "—can be yours."

"I can't wait to make editor."

"It'll happen." Her assurances meant more to me than she knew. "Just give it time and a few more bylines."

Her face fell a little, and she peered up at me. "Everything is good with Braden, too, I take it?" She grabbed my hand.

I sighed and tried to answer her as best I could. Truth was, I didn't know where Braden and I were. Things had been so strained the past few days. "We made up. I'm just not sure if he's completely over everything."

She squeezed my fingers. "Are you?"

I wanted to say yes, that I would forgive and forget and not think about it anymore. But I could still hear his words in my head—about how baseball was the only thing he cared about. Forgiving him was one thing. Forgetting was something else entirely. "I'm working on it." It was all I could manage and still be truthful.

"It will all work out. You two are great together. It's just a rough patch right now. And you did a great thing by forgiving him. Really." Her warm green eyes held so much concern for me that I had to will myself to slap on a smile instead of tearing up.

"I know it'll all work out. You're right."

She dropped my hand and patted me on the ass—just the way I liked. Then her tone turned back to business. "Now, the key to making editor is to, one, produce great content, and two, keep producing great content. So what's your next story idea?"

I walked back to her love seat and sat on the arm. "I haven't really thought of anything."

"Then that's your next goal. Think of a new topic—something fresh and fun—and bring it to me. We'll talk it over and, if it's a go, you can pitch it to Graciela like you did last time." She turned back to her computer and poised her fingers over her keyboard.

"A new topic." I chewed my lip, trying to think of something that would interest *Style and Substance* readers.

"Get to it. I'll send your piece on over to copy editing and let you know what Graciela says, if she doesn't let you know herself." She gave me one more smile. "I'm proud of you on all fronts."

"Thanks, bestie."

"Any time, bestie."

I left her office feeling better about my career. She'd given me concrete feedback and shown me the way forward.

My love life didn't get such direct instructions, but I held on to her assurances that Braden and I belonged together, no matter what.

CHAPTER TEN

BRADEN

IT WAS THE BOTTOM of the ninth, and I found myself in the same position I was in the last time I fucked up the game. There were runners on second and third, and we were down by one run. The opposing team's coach had just called in their closer, and he was warming up. I strolled over to Coach.

"Just do what you did last time. The guy got lucky. You played it right." Coach spit some sunflower seeds into the grass.

"I know."

"Good. Well go win the fucking game then." He swatted me on the ass.

"At least cup the balls if you're gonna spank me, Coach." I winked at him as I walked away toward the plate.

He starts three out of four hitters with a first pitch slider. Eight out of nine who bat my spot in the order.

I always did my homework. I'd studied this guy over and over. Charts, pitch selections—every piece of information we had. If he threw that slider where I wanted, I knew exactly what to do with it.

I stepped into the batter's box, and the crowd came alive around me.

"Crush this shit, B!"

I wasn't sure how Easton's voice always made it above the crowd, but I could always hear it from the dugout. With both of my feet planted in the soft dirt, it was time to go to

77

work.

Focus.

The pitcher came set and everything disappeared but the two of us. I wasn't losing today.

He kicked his leg up to his chin and exploded off of his back leg toward the plate.

Slider. Slider.

His arm whipped around, and he released the ball. It was the pitch I wanted.

I rolled my shoulders back and took an inside-out swing just as the ball broke sharp toward the outside corner.

I smashed it.

It was a hard shot down the first base line. I dropped the bat and sprinted toward the bag as the first baseman laid out, reaching for the ball. It cleared his glove by a matter of inches and curved hard. It landed roughly two feet inside the foul line and then bounced into the right field corner.

Air rushed into my lungs as I sprinted toward first. The crowd thundered around me.

What the fuck? I felt a soft pop in my knee and I stumbled, suspended in the air like I was in slow motion, before planting face first in the chalk line.

I raised my head up to see the right fielder scoop up the ball next to the foul pole. My teammate that was on second was rounding third and heading for the plate to score the winning run. But there were two outs, and I had to make it to first base, or the game was over. We'd lose.

I sprang to my feet and a dull pain radiated from my thigh down to my toes.

The front office is watching. An injury and they will cut you for sure.

I ran as hard as I could to first base, somehow fighting through the pain ripping through my leg. The right fielder fired the ball toward first base, knowing that throwing me out was their last chance at getting the win. I leapt for the bag just as the ball arrived.

I couldn't see anything above me as I stared at the base

and stretched my arms as far out as humanly possible. My fingers slid over the top of the hard plastic, and my body followed right behind. Unable to see the umpire, I listened for the crowd to tell me if I'd made it in time.

A split second seemed like a thousand years. Then the place went fucking insane.

Safe.

I clapped my hands out in front of my face, sending a dusty dirt cloud straight up my nose. Adrenaline coursed through my veins, and I hoped it would carry me off the field without limping. I had to keep everything normal until I could figure out what to do about my knee.

My teammates were rushing after me, smiles plastered to their faces, some of them screaming and jumping.

Fuck a goddamn duck.

I had to play it just right. If they tackled me they might fuck up my knee worse, but if I didn't let them, the front office would know I was possibly injured. Easton was in the front of the pack and I locked eyes with him. I glanced to my knee, before holding my hand up slightly to let him know to slow down when he got to me.

He nodded.

When the stampede arrived, Easton took me to the ground, and I landed with my bad knee in the air to avoid impact. He propped himself on all fours over my knee and took the entire weight of the dog pile onto his back. How he did it, I had no idea.

We were face to face. "Nice fucking rip, man."

"Thanks, buddy." I strained to lift my head toward his ear. "Help me as much as you can, but don't let anyone see."

"Okay."

After a few moments, the dog pile finally cleared, and Easton helped me to my feet. My knee was pretty fucked, but it could easily just be a bad bruise that would heal on its own in a day or two. I'd play through it like usual. The shit happened to catchers all the time.

While surrounded by all the guys, Easton kept his arm out for me to hold onto for support as I walked. When we were about ten feet from the dugout, everyone scattered, and I nodded at him.

He let go. I gritted my teeth and walked the last ten feet to the dugout on my own like nothing was wrong. It hurt so fucking bad I couldn't even look at Nik. That crushed me more than anything.

Easton and Coach stood in front of me after most of the players had gone. People had big mouths, and I couldn't risk any information getting back to the GM.

Once sure everyone had left, Coach turned to me. "How bad?"

"It's not that bad, Coach."

"The fuck." Easton drew out his syllables, and he turned to Coach. "I had to take the weight of the pile so they didn't land on him. And then help him off the field until the guys scattered. I still don't know how he walked the last ten feet like that. He didn't even look at his girlfriend, so I *know* it's worse than 'not that bad.'" He shook his head. "You can fucking trust us. We're on your side. But you need to tell the truth. Stop trying to shoulder everything."

Coach folded his arms over his chest and scowled. "He's right you know? For once."

"Oh, eat me." Easton chuckled, as did I.

"Look, it could be bad. It could be bruised. I don't know." I pulled off a cleat.

"Did you feel a pop?" asked Easton.

I dropped my gaze to the ground.

Easton ran both hands up behind his head, and he arched his back as he looked up. "He has to go to a doctor."

"Fuck you." I tried to stand up and hobbled for a second.

"I'm not going to a doctor. Ain't happening!"

"Boys. Calm the fuck down. This shit doesn't solve anything."

Easton paced back and forth. "He felt a pop. You heard him. His knee—"

"What's that about a knee?"

The three of us turned our heads in the direction of the voice. Rick Ingram, the general manager of the team, walked in. He was mid-thirties and the smuggest fuck on the planet. He'd been a big time sports analyst, and had devised a system using math and statistics to value baseball players. He saw us as numbers, not people, and gave no points for any intangibles like leadership or character. He was a cunt-o-potamus rex.

"Huh?" Coach's voice boomed as Ingram strolled over.

"I heard something about a knee. What's up? You okay, Braden?" A devilish smile formed on Ingram's face.

"Just fine, sir." I prayed he wouldn't ask me to stand. I needed ice in the worst way, and then a whirlpool soak, and then for Nik to sit on my dick. Then I'd be fine.

"VanDerbakken."

We all stared at Coach.

"What?" He shrugged. "He tore his ACL last week. Catcher for the A's. That's who we were talking about."

It was true. I'd read about it a couple days ago.

"Oh, right." Ingram brushed off the sleeve of his suit with distaste. He acted as if he hated having to come down and mingle with his lowly players. He turned his stare from Braden to Coach, and he motioned toward Coach's office.

"Yep. You guys behave. But enjoy the win. Great fucking hit, Braden. You really *saved* our asses tonight. I don't know what we'd do without you." Coach glowered at Ingram as he spoke, then stomped over to his office.

Finally, they shut the door and I whipped my head up to meet Easton's stare. "Get me out of here, quick."

CHAPTER ELEVEN
NIKKI

"I WISH I COULD get in bed with you." I sighed and fastened the back to my earring. My mom had called and invited me, just me, for dinner again. I'd refused. Then she sent my dad, who claimed my mom wanted to apologize, to visit me at work. Worry had laced his voice and crinkled his forehead. The scene the prior week had them on edge about Braden.

I couldn't hide from Mom forever, unfortunately, so I intended to get it over with. Maybe they'd listen to me if I could talk to them one on one. Braden was going to be a part of my life with or without them. I just had to make them understand.

"You look beautiful." Braden placed his hands behind his head.

I twirled so he could see all of me. My white top draped along my breasts, and my navy skirt fell to the middle of my thigh.

He made an *mmm* sound. "Good enough to eat. Speaking of that, come sit on my face."

I arched a brow at him and put in my other earring. "You are having a majorly lazy day. Have you even been out of bed? You're in the same spot you were in when I left for work."

He shifted lower so he was lying flat on his back. "Come on over. I haven't shaved in a couple days either. So this is officially a mustache ride."

I giggled and walked through the bathroom and into the closet to find some shoes.

"I'm serious," he called.

"No, you aren't. You're just trying to make me later than

I already am." I snagged a pair of strappy, silver sandals and returned to the bedroom.

"If you don't get over here, I'll drag you." He raised up on an elbow and gave me a smoldering stare that went straight to my pussy. His broad chest was covered with a light dusting of dark hair, and the covers had slid down to reveal his muscled abs. The sheet began to tent over his cock.

I licked my lips and rubbed my thighs together. "Braden—"

"Tell me no again and you'll get a spanking. Then you'll have to explain to Mommy and Daddy why you can't sit down at dinner."

My knees went weak. "Oh my God. You're awful."

He leaned back and grinned. "Yes, yes I am. Now get that pussy on my face."

My nipples hardened painfully against the molded cups of my bra. I wanted a spanking, of course, but I also wanted to be able to sit normally when I met with my parents. Then again, it seemed obvious that, when faced with having my pussy eaten or not having my pussy eaten, I should always go with having my pussy eaten. Even if it made me late to dinner.

"Nikki—"

"Okay, okay." I slid my panties to the floor and walked to the bed. Before I could climb on top, Braden grabbed me around the waist and lifted me onto his chest.

He shoved my skirt up to my hips and stared between my legs. "I'm starving."

"Braden." I put a hand to my throat, my heart suddenly beating too fast.

"Show me your tits." He grabbed my ass and pulled me toward the head of the bed.

I moved my knees so they were above his shoulders, my pussy hovering right above his face. He wrenched the fabric of my skirt tight around my stomach and stared up at me as I lifted my shirt and pulled my bra down. My pussy tingled each time he exhaled, and goosebumps rose all over my skin as he stared at my tits.

"Pinch your nipples." He kneaded my ass.

I did as he said, pinching my nipples and moaning from my own touch.

"That's my good girl." He wrapped his hands around my upper thighs and pulled me down onto his mouth.

"Oh, Jesus." My head fell back when he licked me from my entrance to my clit. I tried to lift up from him a little, to give him some space.

He wasn't having it. His hands tightened on my thighs, pulling my full weight down onto him as he growled into my wet skin. He licked again and stopped.

I peered down at him, and he began swirling his tongue around my clit, but when I looked at the headboard, he stopped.

"You want me to watch?" I pinched my nipples harder and rocked my hips against his lips as he nodded.

I kept my gaze locked on his as he pressed his tongue inside me. His kissing skills translated well from my mouth to my pussy. I cupped my tits and let my hips go, riding his face in long, slow movements.

He increased his tempo, focusing on my most sensitive spot and gripping my thighs hard enough to leave bruises.

Each swipe of his tongue sent a jolt of pleasure through me, and tension pooled low in my hips. My movements became shorter and faster as he ran the broadside of his tongue against my clit again and again. I closed my eyes for a moment. When he stopped, I wanted to slap him. Instead, I opened my eyes. The skin around his eyes crinkled as he smiled against me and began licking again.

"Fucker." I glared and then squealed as he popped my ass with a smack.

He intensified his efforts, and I rode him hard, the way he liked it. I ground my pussy down on him, giving him every bit of me to lick and suck. My thighs began to tremble, and I kept my gaze firmly fixed on his hazel eyes. He did that thing where he flicked me with the tip of his tongue, then bore down and sucked. I was gone, moaning low in my throat as my hips seized and I came with a thumping orgasm. He shook his head back and forth, sending tiny explosions rocketing through my body until every circuit was overloaded. I leaned against the headboard and finally closed my eyes.

He licked a few more times, then scooted my hips down a little and grinned up at me.

"You go on to your parents' house and get some grub. I'm all good here."

"You. Are. Ridiculous." I said between pants. I wanted to kiss him, but 'contortionist' wasn't in my repertoire.

"Nope. Just full of delicious pussy." He ran his hands across my ass and gave my mound a hard kiss. "And if they ask, feel free to tell your parents I already ate."

"Braden didn't mind fending for himself for dinner, did he?" Mother asked with faux concern as we sat down at the table.

I couldn't stop the smile that spread across my face. "He did just fine. Don't worry."

"I hate that I missed the chance to meet him." Ben, my older brother, smiled warmly at me. I hadn't realized how much I'd missed him. He worked in a bigger city a few hours away and rarely came home.

"You'll meet him soon. Maybe you can come to a game with me?"

"That would be awesome. Do you get good seats?" His light brown hair needed a cut, but he was otherwise well put-together in a simple button-down and jeans.

"The best. Right behind home plate." I smiled, warming at the thought of having an ally at the table.

"Count me in."

My father cleared his throat and leaned forward, elbows on the table. "Speaking of Braden, we'd like to talk about what happened. Your mother and I need to know what sort of future you see with him."

Way to start the heavy shit as early as possible. I placed my napkin in my lap as the cook set the salad course in front of me. "I see a long future with him."

My mother coughed dryly, but I continued, "He's the only man I've ever felt this way about. I'm in love with him. Whenever I think about him, I smile." As if on cue, the corners of my lips turned up at the thought of the orgasm he'd given me before I'd left the apartment. "We argue sometimes, sure. We have tiffs like the one here. Though, in his defense, he was goaded into that." I shot a pointed look at my mother, who avoided my gaze. "But we always make up. We're always there for each other. He's the one."

"But he has a temper." My father speared a piece of lettuce.

I crossed my arms. "Not really. That scene, caused by *Carter*, was completely out of character for him."

"Are you saying I missed a scene?" Ben ran a hand through his hair and chuckled. "Why do I always miss the good stuff?"

I nodded. "Mom decided she would invite Carter over for dinner at the same time I was bringing Braden to meet them."

"Mom." Ben slung his arm around her shoulders and squeezed. "Come on, you know that wasn't cool."

He'd always had a way with her. Maybe it was because he was the oldest or maybe because he was a boy, but Mom always caved when it came to Ben. Relief began to surge inside me just from knowing he was on my side.

She pursed her lips. "Well, I just thought—"

"You're too smart for your own good." He squeezed her again before going back to his salad. "So, if Carter and Braden were here together, of course there was some sort of a fight, right?"

Despite Ben's efforts, Mom seemed undeterred. "Braden isn't the sort of man I pictured you with. He's so, so angry. And he's uneducated."

"He knows what he needs to know to succeed at baseball. That's his career." I shrugged.

"But what will he do after his career is over?" My father's eyes softened, and he put a hand on my upper arm. "He's got what, five good years of baseball left, if that? His knees will go eventually. It happens to all catchers. Then what's his plan? You've always been a hard worker, setting goals and knocking them down. Mom told me how you're writing an article for *Style and Substance* now, already moving up. You have a bright future. We're so proud of you. We just want to make sure you aren't chaining yourself to someone who doesn't share your work ethic."

I fidgeted in my seat. Braden and I had never talked about what his plans were after baseball. Did he have some sort of backup career? What *would* he do when the seasons were over? Dad withdrew his hand, and the room fell silent as the cook replaced our salad plates with the main course— prime rib, roasted vegetables, and baked potatoes.

"He'll find something else after baseball. We'll figure it out together." My voice had lost some of its strength, but I tried to sit a little taller to make up for it. "That's how we do everything. Together."

Dad cut into his prime rib and made an "oomph" noise. Mom shifted in her seat, and I suspected she'd kicked him under the table.

He began, "You know, I'm still involved in certain baseball circles." He glanced at Mom but continued, "I was talking to a friend of the Ravens GM the other day after a round of golf at the club. He mentioned that Braden might be traded. Has he discussed that with you?"

Mom couldn't contain her triumphant smile. I'd wipe that right off for her.

"We've discussed it. It's one of the reasons he was so

upset the other night. The trade talks were weighing on him. Maybe if you'd treated him like a person instead of some sort of insect you needed to brush away, he would have shared that information." I was telling the truth, mostly. I didn't mention that he hadn't even told me until we were standing in the front yard and he was yelling at me. I winced at the memory. I'd resolved to forgive him for it, to try and forget it. But it still hurt all the same.

Mom's smile fell away, and at least I got a slice of satisfaction from dousing her smugness.

"And that's why he yelled—"

"Wait." Ben's eyes narrowed. "He yelled at you?"

"Just a little. Nothing crazy."

Mom's smile was back.

Ben pinched the bridge of his nose. "'Just a little'? He's lucky I don't kick his ass! No guy yells at you, understand?"

I stared at him. "You're yelling right now."

"I'm your brother!" He clanged his fork on his plate. "I get to yell when you act like an idiot and let some guy walk all over you."

Ben was so even-keeled that his anger took me off guard.

I needed him on my side. "It wasn't like that. When you meet him, you'll see. I promise, he's never yelled before. It was just that one time."

"One time too many," Ben grumbled.

"Please have some faith in me. I would never be with a guy who mistreated me, okay?" I tucked my hair behind my ears and stared down at my plate as tears burned behind my eyes. My parents? I could handle their disapproval. But my brother, too?

Ben took a deep breath and, in a calmer voice, asked, "So, where are they thinking of sending him?"

He was throwing me a bone. I'd take it and run with it. "He doesn't know. They haven't actually sat down and discussed it yet. There will be a meeting next week, I think."

I picked at my food and tried to regain the same confidence I had when I left the apartment, fully satisfied with myself and my boyfriend.

"Are you okay with leaving your job, though?" Ben asked. "Especially now that you're getting more responsibilities? Doesn't it bother him that he'll be taking you away from all that?"

"He hasn't …" My fingers went cold as I realized what I was about to say. "He hasn't asked me to go with him." My voice was small, almost as small as I felt.

"Thank God." My mother drained her glass and motioned for another.

Disappointment hit me so hard in the chest that I thought it might bruise. Even after Braden and I had made up and discussed the trade issue, he'd never asked if I'd go with him. He'd talked about places he didn't want to go or teams he wouldn't mind joining. He'd even discussed the costs of moving all his things. But never once did he ask, or even mention, that I'd be at his side.

"Nik, you okay?" Ben placed his napkin next to his plate and rose.

"Yes, I'm fine." I stood and held out my palm toward him. "Stay, finish your meal. I'm not feeling so great. I think I'll go."

"Nikki, please stay." Dad's pleading tone joined Ben's concerned look and made my insides heave. They pitied me, and it almost broke me down to tears. I couldn't let it.

I straightened my back, wiped an errant tear from my cheek, and strode toward the front door. "I can't. I have something I need to do."

CHAPTER TWELVE

BRADEN

I HEARD A RATTLING against the door handle. "Fuck me. Nik's home early." Grabbing the remote, I clicked the power button and turned the TV on. The laptop tumbled over onto the floor, and the wireless mouse rolled under the coffee table. "Son of a fuck."

I shot back against the cushion, doing my best to act normal. Nik pushed the door open. "Hey, babe. I was waiting for my dessert course." I made a show of scrubbing my hand across my mouth and face like I was clearing her a space.

"I'm good." Her tone was flat, and she didn't even look at me.

What the hell?

Her usual spark was gone. She sauntered over to the side table, and dropped her keys and bag on it.

I glanced down at the laptop screen full of porn. *Fuck!* I'd been researching some new shit to try out with her, but there was no way she'd believe me. My gaze drifted to the mouse way up under the table. There was no chance I could get to it without giving away my knee situation.

Using my good leg, I tried to gently kick the computer screen closed, and, of course, it only opened wider.

"Have you moved from the couch all night? Did you even shower?" She sighed, still facing the wall like she had no interest in looking at me.

"What's wrong, babe? What happened?" My mind raced.

A lot could have occurred at Estate de CuntMuffin that would set her off. I'd been worried the whole time she was gone.

"I'm fine." She turned around, and I watched her eyes dart straight to the computer screen. Her brows pinched together and her hands went to her hips.

Fuck me. This won't be good.

"Nice, Braden. Real fucking nice."

"It's not what you think. I don't look at porn." I stared in the other direction and mumbled. "Often."

"Your fingers slip and accidentally type in 'fuckmedaddy.com?'" She scowled and began to pace back and forth.

I'd expected her to be upset about the porn, but not this much. I was halfway hoping she'd want to look at it with me. "No. I was trying to find new stuff to try out on you. If you must know."

Her lips curled like she might smile, and then they mashed back into a thin line.

So close.

"Have they said if you're going to be traded or not?" She took another step toward me, ignoring all of the pussy acrobatics flashing on the laptop.

"No." I tilted my head to my lap and ground my teeth while I tried to compose myself. I'd been trying to forget about that shit all day, but the pain in my knee kept it front and center in my mind.

She made a *pfft* sound and threw her arms in the air.

"Babe, I'm sorry. I know I'm supposed to have a clue what you're upset about. I just don't."

A million things rocketed through my mind at once and brought my entire thought process to a crashing halt. My brain buffered slower than the inverted cowgirl pussy nomming scene I'd attempted to watch earlier.

Nik scowled, and then folded her arms across her chest. She stared me down like a closer in the ninth inning. "Think really really hard about the problem we have."

My eyes rolled up toward the ceiling. "Uhh, your parents?" I glanced back and tried to judge her reaction.

She made a loud sound like a buzzer that startled me.

"Fucking hell. I mean, umm, me being traded?" I held my hands up and shrugged.

"Warmer." She took another step toward me.

I hated this fucking guessing game. Why couldn't she just say it? Heat rushed into my face, and my body tensed.

"Can you just tell me? Please. Stop fucking around with me." I smacked my hand against the back of the sofa, and Nik jumped.

"Maybe my parents were right. Maybe you do have anger issues." She stomped off a few steps and whipped back around. "*Easton!*"

"Take that shit back. You know I don't. Maybe your goddamn family just brings it out of everyone. Maybe you're more like your mo—" I froze stiff on the couch, and my eyes bugged out. I held up my hands. "I stopped myself. You heard me. I did not say it."

It was too late. I thought my head was going to explode the way Nik glowered in my direction. Her hands were squeezed into fists at her sides, and I could see all the whites of her knuckles. She started toward me like a possessed demon. "Did you say what I think you said?"

Do not answer, Braden. That shit is rhetorical. Adapt and survive.

I shook my head quickly and braced myself in case she resorted to physical violence.

When she was about three feet away, I covered my face with my hands. I waited, and nothing happened. I peeked between my fingers, and she stood in front of me.

Her words came through gritted teeth. "Through all your bullshit pity party, and your fucking blow-up at my parents—"

"That wasn't all my—"

She held up her hand, and I shut the fuck up immediately.

"You've wallowed around and discussed moving your

shit, packing your shit, cities you are okay with, places you won't go—but you never once asked me to go with you."

"Babe, I—" I closed my mouth.

She didn't let me speak, and wouldn't believe me now if I tried.

"You said baseball is all you've got. You made that very clear to me, Braden. And you know what? You're absolutely right." She turned on her heel, and I watched as she walked out the door.

Jumping up to my feet to chase her, pain ripped through my knee and shot down my leg. I stumbled for a second and then beefed it face-first onto the carpet. I stared around at my house from the floor, looking up at everything I owned. Nothing in my life meant shit without her. I'd definitely hit rock bottom. Of course I wanted her to go with me. It was a given. I figured she just knew that. That's if I even had to leave at all. I bounced my forehead on the floor. My entire life was falling apart over a hypothetical situation.

I had to talk to someone. I hobbled to the table and grabbed my phone. Flicking through my contacts, I stared at the only girl I could talk to about shit like this. I cringed as I tapped Kasey's number.

"Aye, what the bloody hell?" Patrick squinted and leaned over the bar to get a good look at me. "Braden? That you?"

The place was empty, as usual, as I hobbled up to a stool. "Yeah. Don't ask." It was darker than normal, which was no surprise to me, considering I had on the blackest pair of sunglasses I could find and a cowboy hat Nik had made me wear to some western-themed party.

"Fuck, son. Y'all right in tha head? Ya walk like someone fucked ya sideways." He tried to hold back a chuckle, and failed.

On any other day I'd have laughed with him, but the pain of Nik leaving was still a dagger in my chest. "Hurt my knee during the game. Can't let anyone know."

He held up an empty pint glass and gestured toward the tap.

"Indeed." I let out a long sigh as I sat down and propped my elbows on the bar top.

The front door swung open. Patrick and I both turned to look.

"What in the—" Kasey doubled over in laughter, pointing right at me. After a few seconds that lasted far too long, she tried to compose herself, but chortled uncontrollably when she tried to speak. "I just can't—" She started toward me, her face reddening more with each step. "What in the Virgin Mary's cunt drapes are you wearing, Doyle Brunson? You been playing Texas Cuckold 'em at the Bellatio spa and resort again?" She doubled over at her own joke.

"Keep them coming. I have all day."

Patrick sat the pint in front of me, and I drank down a few large gulps.

"Okay. I'm done." She leaned over and examined my glasses and the hat. "I had a great one about Chokeback Mountman, but you ruined it with your Debbie Downer ways. Now, why am I here?"

"I need advice. Shit happened between me and Nik." I stared down into my glass and watched the tiny bubbles float around.

Her brow furrowed. "Why does everyone think I'm the Dr. Phil of pussy around here?"

Patrick chuckled in the corner. He usually tried to stay out of our conversations, but Kasey was loud enough for the whole damn city to hear. Kasey turned to him. "Hey there, lover. Sorry for being rude and not saying hi. I was distracted by Sideshow Bob over here. Can you say 'fuck ass' for me once?" She grinned.

"I'd do anything for you, love." He polished a rocks glass

with his bar towel. "But I won't do that."

"You Meatloafin' son-of-a-bitch, you." Kasey's eyes flitted back to me.

I grumbled. "Can you fucking focus for two seconds?"

"What'd you do?"

"Why do you assume I'm the one at fault?" I yanked my sunglasses from my face and sat my hat on the counter.

"You risked going in public looking like that to talk to me. You definitely fucked up bad."

"Fair point. First, I'm wearing the stupid shit because I hurt my knee the other night. I don't need people taking pictures of me hobbling around town. Ingram doesn't know about it. Secondly, during all the bullshit that's gone down, I never specifically asked Nikki if she'd go with me if I was traded."

Kasey's jaw flexed and I leaned away from her, thinking she might punch the shit out of me. "You did what?"

"I just assumed she would. I mean we're together, right? I figured that keeps going unless we break up."

She muttered under her breath. "Idiot."

"Look, Kase. She left me. I'm miserable. How do I get her back?"

"You men make it so easy for me, I swear. If I didn't like you, I'd have her legs spread like wings tonight while I dined in first-class. So, fate is on your side." She tilted her head back to stare up for a moment, and then returned her gaze to me. Her eyes opened wider, as if a light bulb went off in her head. "You need a grand gesture."

"Well, I thought about like flowers and a card."

My head whipped to the side when she smacked me above my ear.

"Don't be a fucking Easton. He's the stupid one. You're a sweet guy. What's this shit I've heard about you blowing up and yelling at people? That isn't you."

What *was* my deal? I thought I had everything under control. But now, I'd lost the woman I loved and was about to lose my job.

"So it needs to be a big gesture, right? With umm, thought behind it? Not just money?"

Kasey began a steady, slow clap and mocked me with her tone. "He has returned from Twatville, ladies and gents. Leaving the ass-bag Easton Holliday as the only remaining resident."

I grinned. "But what should I do? As a gesture?"

Kasey rubbed her chin. "I have an idea."

CHAPTER THIRTEEN
NIKKI

"DARLING." MOM SANK ONTO my bed and patted my thigh. "While I'm glad to have you home for the weekend, I wish you weren't having so many problems with that Braden."

I squinted against the morning light and did my best to glare at her. "Things were going fine until you threw Carter in his face." My voice faltered when I realized my words weren't true. Things hadn't been fine ever since Braden's season started going south. Instead of sharing his problems or fears with me, he'd turned inward. Now, I was sleeping in my old room, ruffle bedspread and all, and he was alone in our apartment. "How did all of this get so fucked up?"

Mom tsked and sipped her coffee, the delicious smell the only thing keeping me from falling apart. I'd wanted to go to Kyrie's after my confrontation with Braden, but I didn't want to be a cock block again. Nothing was worse than a cock block, except for maybe a monumental cock tease. I may have committed the former a time or two, but never the latter.

I pressed my head down into my pillow and pulled my blanket over my face. "Just go away."

"Despite what you think, I want to help. Your father and I are worried about you. Can you just…" She sighed. "Can you just take a little break from him maybe? See what else is out there?"

Tears stung behind my eyes and I shook my head. My

warm breath filled the small pocket beneath the blanket, but I'd rather suffocate than cry over a boy in front of my mom. "I told you. He's it for me."

She pulled the blanket from my face and ran her hand over my cheek. The kind gesture spurred more tears. I was turning into an emotional wreck.

She swiped a tear from the corner of my eye. "I know, Nik. I do. But are you it for him?"

There was no sting in her words, none of the usual conniving, only concern. *Resolve broken.* I sat up and hugged her as more tears coursed down my cheeks. She set her coffee cup on my bedside table and wrapped her arms around me.

"I thought I was. I thought he loved me. But he's been acting so strange lately. He's so angry, and I don't know what to do to fix it."

"He hasn't hurt you, has he?"

"No." One thing I was sure of was that he'd never raise a hand to me. The opposite was more likely. When he left his shaving gunk—including gooey shaving cream peppered with the tiny hairs from his face—in the sink two weeks ago, I had a vivid mental image of punching him out. "I'm not afraid of him. I've threatened to cut off his dick in his sleep before, and he didn't bat an eyelash."

She tittered out a small laugh. "I'm not surprised. You've always been ... let's just say, *fiery.*"

"I've been called worse." I sniffled. "I just don't understand him right now."

She smoothed a hand down my hair, her familiar scent of lavender and pricey Scotch comforting me more than anything else could. "I miss this." Her words were soft, barely a whisper.

"I miss you, too." I squeezed her tight and wiped my face all over her luxury bath robe.

"Nik!"

"What?" I laughed. "Terry cloth is made for snot and tears, very absorbent and stuff."

She pushed me out to arm's length and shook her head, her usual pinched look replacing the much-needed softness. "What am I going to do with you?"

"You're going to let me make my own mistakes." I flopped back down into bed and stared up at the recently hand-painted ceiling. Mom had decided to make the house "feel more French." As a result, fat little cherubs smiled down at me, likely fantasizing about jizzing all over me while I slept. It didn't matter. I was fucked with or without an angelic bukkake.

She followed my gaze to the overdone mural. "You like what Jacques did? I think it looks elegant."

"I liked it better when it was simple." Problem was, I didn't know if I was talking about the Jizztine Chapel overhead or my relationship with Braden.

"This is so not my color." I spun in the dressing room mirrors, all three reflecting the pink confection of a dress my mother had picked.

Over the years, the Graves had suffered plenty of hardships—when the good caviar was out of season, when that one maid failed to do proper hospital corners when she made the beds, or even that time when Kerfuffles, Mom's prized Dandie Dinmont Terrier, destroyed my father's autographed baseball from the '56 World Series where Don Larsen threw a perfect game. Each time there was a setback, the Graves rallied in the only way we knew how. We shopped.

I wasn't into it like Mom, but if buying me new clothes got her off my back about Braden—and finally gave me some breathing room—I was all for it. I couldn't go back to the apartment, not until I knew what my course of action would be. So, a day of shopping didn't sound so bad while I mulled things over.

"I think you look lovely in it." My mother walked around, her critical eye examining it from every angle.

"What will I wear it to? My *quinceañera?*"

"I'm sure you have plenty of weddings to attend next spring. In this, you'll outshine the bride." She smiled.

"Yes, Mom, because my goal is always to ruin the bride's special day by flouncing around in a sherbet-colored dress and flashing my panties at all the boys, including the groom." I stepped down from the modeling podium and walked into my separate changing area. I didn't mention that I had, on plenty of occasions, bagged a groomsman or two at my friends' weddings, often using similar tactics to what I just described.

Mom gave an over-dramatic sigh. "Stop being difficult, and try on the next dress."

"This one is the newest from the Valentino line." The snooty shopping assistant reassured my mother that she was, for certain, buying the most expensive shit in all of Saks. "I wish I could have been at the runway show. It was faboosh, beyond transcendentine, positively luxotic."

"Those aren't words," I muttered and fought the zipper on my mother's next selection. This one wasn't so bad. It was a sky blue sheath that fell mid-thigh and had an interesting peasant-top ruffle at the bust line.

I walked out and stood on the podium as the assistant—a man wearing more makeup than I owned—flittered about and crowed about the fit.

Mom took a swig of the complimentary champagne. "Cyrano, she looks like a barmaid."

I smiled at myself in the mirror. "It's my favorite one so far. Tit-tastic." If a dress made it look like I had actual breasts that were bigger than a teacup, then I was sold.

"An excellent choice. The bodice is ahead of its time. I have a feeling peasant will be in three years from now." Cyrano—if that was actually his name—twirled one side of his too-thick mustache and affected a lisp that screamed "flamer." But he wasn't fooling me. I'd seen him checking out my tits and ass while I modeled my dresses. He was straight, but likely knew that pretending to like the dick was the surest way to get commissions in a Saks dressing room.

Let's test this theory. I smirked and headed back into the changing area. After yanking my zipper halfway down, I called, "My zipper is stuck. Cyrano, a little help?"

He pushed through the white curtain and let it fall behind him. His eyes took in my bare back and bra strap.

"I can't quite get it." I smiled at him in the mirror.

"Allow me, mademoiselle." He gripped the zipper and pulled it down easily. "There we are."

I let the dress fall to the floor and turned to face him. His gaze froze on my tits, then lowered to the lace over my pussy.

I plucked at the edge of my panties, pulling them away from my hip. Then I looked at him through my lashes. "Do you think I'd have to go without panties in that dress. Did you see a line?"

He licked his lips. "I-I think—" His voice had lowered two octaves in the space of ten seconds.

When I saw his boner at war with the front of his skinny pants, I laughed. "So busted. Quit ogling my pussy, and go entertain my mom."

"What?" He cleared his throat and raised his voice into a nasal pitch again. "Oh, vaginas are so icky. I would never—"

"Tell it to your boner." I crossed my arms over my chest and gave his crotch a pointed stare.

He dropped the act. "Look, I make good money this way, okay? When I played it straight, women never took my style advice. Style is my life, and this is the only way I can be around it and make money at it. Please don't say anything."

Guilt filtered through me, and I dropped my arms. "I'm not judging. Well, I'm not now, anyway. I was just messing with you."

He smiled a little. "What gave me away?"

"Your roving eye."

103

"I've been trying to work on that, but when I see a beautiful woman." He gestured at me. "I can't help it sometimes."

An idea struck me like a wild pitch. "You get the inside scoop on designer clothes and what the customers come in here looking for all the time, right?"

He ran his thumbs up and down his bright pink suspenders. "Yeah. It's kind of my job."

"I'll tell you what—wait, what's your name?"

"Cyrano."

I rolled my eyes. "No, your *real* name."

His shoulders drooped. "Cyrus."

"Okay, Cyrus. You agree to let me interview you for my magazine, and I won't tell everyone what a true pussy-fiend you are. Sound like a deal?"

"Magazine?" He twirled his mustache.

"I work for *Style and Substance.*"

His eyes lit up, and he grabbed my upper arms. "Are you shitting me?"

I shook my head. "Not even a little shitting. Not so much as a shart."

"Yes!" He nearly shouted. Then he ran his hands down my arms. "Sorry about that. It's just, that's my favorite fashion mag. It's so down-to-earth but also classy beyond belief."

His enthusiasm had my mind whirling in all different directions, but first things first.

"Good." I plucked one of his business cards from the front pocket of his plaid shirt. "I'll be in touch, *Cyrano.*"

After Mom bought the ruffle dress and then guilted the *quinceañera* dress on me, despite my protests, we finally left Saks and meandered around some other high-end shops. She picked out some obscenely expensive bags and shoes, then we stopped to eat at one of the upscale restaurants within the shopping center.

"We have a reservation. Graves." Mom handed her bags to the maître d, as if it were perfectly acceptable to treat restaurant staff like bell hops.

He paused for a moment, then took her bags and passed them off to another server for safekeeping. "Right this way, Mrs. Graves."

We followed him through a sea of tables covered in white cloths and fresh floral arrangements.

"One of your number has already arrived." He stepped aside and showed us to a table. Carter sat facing me, his eyes traveling down the length of my body.

Irritation rose inside me, and I hissed into Mom's ear, "What the hell are you doing?"

"Having lunch." She took the only chair across the round table from Carter, forcing me to either sit at his side or skip lunch. Since option two simply wasn't something I was prepared to do, I grabbed the chair next to Carter and yanked it away from him. I sat between the two of them, not sure who I should glare at the hardest.

"You look beautiful." Carter gave a self-satisfied smile. He wore a light green button-down shirt, the collars cuffed to give an air of ease.

Instead of relaxed, I was on edge. I ordered a glass of wine from the first server I saw and settled in to play the silent game.

"How was shopping?"

I stared at him, my lips pressed together in childish rebellion. It may have been juvenile, but it felt so good to see his cheery demeanor fade each second I refused to respond.

Mom cut in, "We found some lovely things. Nikki has a few new dresses, and one was particularly gorgeous on her. Pink has always been her color."

Carter smirked. "I've always liked pink, too, especially since Nikki wears it so well." He smoothed his hand along my thigh under the table.

Mom, completely oblivious, took a drink of her wine as our server placed a small loaf of baguette on the table.

I slapped Carter's hand away and stood. It hurt to give up on a free lunch, but I couldn't deal with them anymore. Their plotting was beginning to feel like a dry dick in my ass.

"I think I'll get a cab home."

"Nikki, darling—"

"No, I've had enough." I grabbed my wine glass and downed it, then snatched the crusty bread and the little butter dish that came with it. Some things were sacred, after all.

I turned and stormed out, ignoring my mother's embarrassed pleas. The shopping center was built like a town center, with cobblestone streets and stores lining each side. As soon as I left, the sun hit me, along with the smell of popcorn and freshly mowed grass. If I closed my eyes, it was as if I were at the ballpark with Braden out in front of me, smiling and going to work. My heart felt suddenly lighter than it had the past few days.

I ripped the bread in half and dug it into the whipped butter before taking a huge bite. The baguette was buttery and warm, and stealing it was by far the best decision I'd made in weeks.

I walked a few more steps and readied to take another bite when a hand gripped my elbow almost painfully. Carter whipped me around, sending my bread and butter flying onto the cobblestones. Unforgiveable.

"Hey, fucker—"

He pressed me into a kiss and wrapped his arms around me, caging me against his body. I yelled into his mouth, and he took the opportunity to sink his tongue deep enough to make me gag.

He bent me backward, and I clutched at him to try and keep my balance. I would knee him as soon as I got the chance, and he would know to never touch me again.

"Nikki?" Braden's voice cut through my anger, and

before I had the chance to use my knee, Carter was on his back.

CHAPTER FOURTEEN

BRADEN

I HOBBLED AROUND THE store, trying to wrap my head around why everything was so expensive.

"Yes, ma'am. Can you tell me about this here Louis Pee Dong number?" Kasey winked at me, and then smiled at the sales lady.

I almost doubled over until my knee buckled. *Fuck*. It wasn't getting any better, and it'd been days since the game.

"It's Louis *Vuitton*, and it's probably out of your price range." The woman snidely told Kasey.

"You're lucky you look hot as balls in that skirt. So I'm going to let that one slide." Kasey waved a flippant hand at the woman and then walked over to me. "You sure this is Nik's favorite shit? It's ugly as fuck and the price of a car. It looks like someone shit Shakespeare font all over the side of it."

"Maybe *your* car," the sales lady muttered and walked back over to the counter.

Kasey's head whipped around. "She's got 'tude. And a hot ass. I'm gonna make her hum 'Louis Vuitton' on the ol' clitty bean later."

"Can you focus? This was your idea. You're going to get us kicked out, and this is the only place that sells Nik's favorite shit." I scowled but wanted to laugh. She was so going to turn that sales lady out later.

"Fine, Braden. Fuckin' A, sir. You're lucky I like you." Kasey walked over to the counter. Though she was the most vulgar person in the entire store, she was also likely the hottest. Tall for a girl, and with blonde hair that plenty of women would kill for, she had a graceful body but a sailor's mouth. I hoped she would turn on the charm and make the entire process smoother.

She leaned against the counter. "What's your name, my pretty?"

The sales lady glanced up. "Gwen." Her tone warmed a bit.

Kasey leaned closer to her, almost conspiratorially. "Lookie here, lovely Gwen. I apologize, for, you know, making fun of your fancy-ass bags, and the name of your store, and a number of other transgressions I've yet to commit. But here's the thing—my friend over there—" she tilted her head toward me, "—he looks like a derelict, hobbling around like a homeless ass-bag. But, he's actually a Major League baseball player who just doesn't know how to dress properly. He had a split with his woman, and he's trying to get her back. Can you help us pick something?" Kase moved closer and whispered something magical, because Gwen's cheeks turned pink before she smiled and walked over to me.

Kasey followed behind her and gave me a thumbs up with a giant smile plastered across her face.

Gwen's heels clacked against the tile floor. I glanced around, wondering what the price of all the bags in the store would add up to.

"So, I understand you're looking for something for a woman?"

How did Kasey always pull this shit off? One minute, women would be disgusted, and the next they were spreading their legs for her.

"Yes, I kind of screwed up."

"Kind of?" She put her hands on her hips.

"I fucked up big, okay? Help me?" I held my hands up as a peace offering, and she grinned.

"Well, I need to know what you're wanting your gift to

express."

"I might be trad—" I paused and collected my thoughts. Trade information wasn't common knowledge, especially amongst the fans. I didn't think the woman knew anything about baseball, but I had to be careful all the same. "We may be traveling a lot. Away games and stuff. I thought if I got her some new luggage, it would suggest I want her to go with me."

"Well, I think that's sweet."

"Like your ass." Kasey was a few feet away running her finger across a bag and checking it for dust.

Gwen's face turned a brighter pink. "Your friend is a trip."

"She's something all right. Anyway, can you help me?" I brushed my clammy hands on my jeans.

"Right this way."

We walked over to a corner where an entire luggage set was on display. She waved a hand through the air, and the pitch in her voice changed to that of a game show announcer. "This is our top-of-the-line collection. She would love this set. It has three different sized trolley cases, travel bag, cosmetic pouch, toiletry kit, and jewelry case. All the highest quality luggage you can own. She would travel in style and turn heads."

I scrubbed a hand over my chin. "What do you think, Kasey?"

Kasey stood there ogling Gwen's ass in her skirt. "Yeah, yeah. Sure."

Fuck me. I'm on my own.

"So what's something like this run?" I shook my head at Kasey, and she shrugged, then I turned back to Gwen.

"This set is twenty thousand, and comes with a lifetime warranty."

I coughed and choked out a few words. "I'm sorry, twenty thousand? American dollars?"

Kasey glared in my direction. "You wanted a grand gesture, right?"

Gwen smiled, as though the lifetime warranty somehow justified the price tag.

I stood there for a moment, staring at all the fucking bags that supposedly would get Nikki back. I turned to Kasey. "You're sure this will work?" I was willing to pay ten times that much if it meant Nik was back in my life and happy.

"Nothing is one hundred percent. But if you still have a shot, this will do it." It was the most serious Kasey had been all day.

"Fuck it. Ring them up."

"Yolo, motherfucker!" Kasey held out a fist.

I tapped my knuckles on hers.

Gwen clapped her hands and practically skipped back to the counter. Kasey seized on the opportunity and smacked her on the ass, eliciting a squeal and a smile.

"This is so romantic." Gwen tapped buttons on a screen with her bright red nails while Kasey leaned on the counter.

"It sure is. I may let you buy me dinner with your lotto winnings from this sale." Kasey looked over at me and hip thrusted the counter while Gwen kept ringing things up.

"I may just take you up on that offer." Gwen smiled, and continued typing in the sales information.

Kasey nudged me and whispered in my ear, "Looks like I'll be nomming the pink taco later."

"Thanks, motherfucker, it only cost me twenty grand." My brows lowered as I glared at her.

"Hey, don't hate on me for piggybacking some sweet pussy love onto the deal. Hater."

"You realize I can hear both of you, right?" Gwen looked up at us.

I pulled out my wallet and handed my credit card to Gwen.

"Oh, don't act like you don't want me to Michael Phelps that pussy." Kasey tossed her golden hair over her shoulder.

I choked. When I looked behind me, there stood a family of four with their mouths agape. Breathing became difficult, and my face had to be bright pink. I whirled back around to catch a look of horror on Gwen's face as Kasey continued to explain the Michael Phelps to her.

"It's like the butterfly swim technique, see? You spread the legs wide, like you're underwater." She whipped both arms out like she just spread a pair of thighs on the counter. "And then you come up and down, like you're swimming for the pink medallion." She bobbed her head up and down as if she was coming up for air, and then diving back down between the hypothetical legs.

Gwen stared at me as if she were pleading for help, and slid my credit card across the counter, along with a receipt to sign. I scribbled my name down as fast as possible and mouthed 'I'm sorry.'

"We'll be going now." The man and his family turned as the wife ear-muffed one of the children.

"Maybe if you Michael Phelps'd your wife once in a while, you wouldn't be in here buying her some goddamn Louis Deepdong luggage. Pfft." Kasey flipped the bird at the man's back as he scooted his family out the front door.

"Yeah, I think we'll be going too. Come on, Kase." I grabbed the handles on Nik's new luggage.

Gwen slid a business card across to Kasey. "Call me."

"Oh, you'll hear from me soon." Kasey scooped up the card and shoved it in her pocket.

"Jesus Christ, you're ridiculous." I started toward the front of the store.

We walked through the glass double doors and out onto the sidewalk. I hobbled along, trying to drag the bags behind while Kasey strolled next to me at a leisurely pace.

"What the hell? You usually love it when I pick up chicks."

"I'm nervous. What if this shit doesn't work? I have to get her back." I noticed a few people staring at me, and I tried to walk as normal as possible, ignoring the sharp pains radiating from my knee.

"Sorry, just trying to lighten the mood a little." Kasey's eyes darted around to the stores as we headed outside to the parking lot.

"Please. You're just trying to tame that pussy in there." I shot her a side eye.

"Oh, is my boyfriend finally getting back to normal? He can talk about pussy again?"

"Boyfriend?"

"Oh yeah, you're my boyfriend when dudes hit on me. I use you as an excuse for anything I don't want to do. I just assumed you'd know that. I love your cock. And your jizz. So, so hard."

I nearly tripped from my sudden loss of focus before righting myself. "Jesus." I shook my head at her while she laughed it up.

We crossed the street to my car and began loading the luggage in the back. "You're a master of your craft. I'll give you that." I leaned over and gave her a peck on the forehead. "Thank you."

She wrapped her arms around my bicep and squeezed. "You're welcome. You know I always got your back."

Her grip on my arm tightened suddenly, and her body tensed. *Weird.* I looked down, and her eyes were wide. She tried to turn and look another way, but I glanced to what she'd been staring at. Nikki was walking out of a restaurant and taking a huge bite of what appeared to be a small loaf of bread. I could have sworn she had a butter dish in her other hand. Typical.

A wave of heat rushed through my limbs when I saw Agent Carter FistFuck walking up behind her. I shook Kasey from my arm and started in that direction.

"Let it go, Braden." Kasey's warning fell on my ears but didn't register.

I heard Kasey's feet pounding the pavement behind me.

"Fuck that. I'm getting to the bottom of this shit right fucking now."

I hobbled across the street, not giving a shit that traffic had to stop for my jay-walk. When I reached the sidewalk, I started for them, bumping anyone in my path out of the way.

I couldn't see Nikki because the tanned yuppie cunt was between us. I was about ten feet away when I watched the arrogant prick kiss Nik, damn near swallowing her face whole. My knee was about to give out, but I didn't give two shits about that or Kasey trying to tug at my arm from behind.

Grabbing him by the back of the collar, I broke their kiss when I yanked him to the ground. I stumbled around in the process, damn near landing face first into the sidewalk myself.

Carter shot to his feet and flashed that shitty cockboy smirk of his. Kasey wedged herself between us.

Carter brushed the front of his shirt. "Oh, look, the jealous stalker boyfriend. What a surprise."

"Shut your mouth, Carter!" Nikki turned to me. "What are you doing here, Braden? Are you following me?" She folded her arms across her chest.

"I was, umm—" I turned my gaze to Kasey who shrugged. "Why the fuck is he kissing you?" I pointed at Captain McGillicunty and his fake-ass surfer tan and blond boy-band hair.

"Wait? That's your ex?" Kasey pointed at Carter and chuckled.

"Something funny, bitch?" Carter glared at Kasey.

Usually, I'd beat his fucking face in, but Kasey would handle that herself shortly. I started to feel sorry for the guy, because he was fucked after that slip of the tongue. My sympathy didn't last long as I awaited the onslaught.

"Oh, no. Did this cunt trap just call me a bitch? Boy, I will fuck your goddamn teeth sideways." She eyed him up and down. "You have a plaid dick, don't you? That shit is two inches and plaid. A toddler noodle. You were just born with it."

Carter stood shell shocked, as both Nik and I tried not to laugh.

Kasey took a step closer. "Your dick is pleated, ain't it? Ol' pleat dick, born ready for a Dockers commercial. How about I shove a polo mallet up your twat gap and use you like a ventriloquist?" Kasey held up her hand like a puppet and spoke out of the side of her mouth. "Help me. Somebody save me from my plaid dick. It's got pleats and everything. Oh wait, maybe those are cunt lips flappin' in the breeze down there. Yep, that's it. I gots pussy pleats. Eff my life."

I was about to burst with laughter when the queen of the Graves household walked out of the restaurant with a stack of dresses draped over one arm.

"Nikki, what is this?" She used that rich-people voice that suggested her daughter was mingling with the commoners again.

I dropped my face into my palm, because I knew what was coming.

"Who the fuck is Lady Godiva Godzilla over here, storming into shit out of nowhere?" Kasey turned to Nik's mom.

Mrs. Graves glared in my direction. "Are you following us? I have high-priced lawyers and we will file protective orders. You can't stalk our daughter."

"I wasn't stalking anyone. It's a public place." I looked down at Nik. "I swear. I wouldn't do that."

"Mmhmm." Carter injected himself back into the conversation.

I ground my teeth together and then turned to Carter. "This doesn't concern you, shit-paper prince. I'll give you a call next time I take a fat Carter in a port-o-potty and run out of ass wipes. Maybe you can do some calculus to solve my problem."

"Nikki's safety concerns me." He walked over and put his arm around her. She stepped away, forcing him to drop his arm to the side. Good girl. But she hadn't stepped toward me like I wanted.

It was like the night in the driveway all over again, me as the bad guy and these assholes filling her ears full of poison about me.

I ignored Carter and Nikki's mom. There was only one person I wanted to talk to. "I'm just going to go. I don't want any problems, Nikki. I want you, but not like this. Just take whatever time you want, and then let me know." I hobbled away, not giving a fuck who saw my limp at that moment.

"You're getting off easy this time, plaid dick." Kasey followed behind me. "Next time I see you, I'm going to lay your ass out and then fuck your girlfriend, if you can get one, anyway."

I ignored the pain in my knee and kept walking, though everything inside me screamed at me to run back to Nikki. But with Carter and her mother around, no good could come of further confrontation.

Kasey's taunting voice rose. "Oh, and Mrs. Snooty-pants, here's a newsflash, that pink dress you're carrying is the ugliest thing I've ever seen. I wouldn't even fuck you if you wore that, Nikki. Just kidding. I'd always fuck you. You know this."

Kasey clapped me on the shoulder as we made it to my car. "My last little bit got her for you. Just wait and see, boyfriend."

CHAPTER FIFTEEN

NIKKI

"FRINGE. IT'S THE BANE of my existence. When it exploded last season, I got so many women requesting it that I almost quit. I can't stand it. Unless you're going to a cowboy festival, don't wear fringe."

I smiled as I typed Cyrus's response. He'd been in my office for the past hour answering questions for my next *Style and Substance* article: "What Your Style Assistant Really Thinks About Your Taste." *Cyrano* would headline the piece. I hoped Cyrus would gain a bigger clientele from giving down and dirty advice in the mag.

Makeup-less and wearing a simple pair of jeans and a black T-shirt, he was a handsome man with excellent taste in clothes. The other assistants had been tittering about him as I'd led him down the hall to my cramped office.

I finished typing his answer and leaned back. "Now, shoot straight with me." I narrowed my eyes. "Off the record. Don't you think that pretending to be gay is, you know, wrong?"

He crossed one leg over the other, resting his ankle on his knee. "Look, my roommate is gay. He's the one who suggested it to me, and then I just ran with it. I know it's not a good thing to do, okay? But if it helps me pay my bills and isn't hurting anyone, why does it matter?"

I scratched my nose. "It just seems so …"

"Dishonest. I know." He craned his head back and sighed. "I'm trying to think of some way to stop, but I kind of can't now. Not at Saks. And now with this article—"

"You could be Cyrus in this article, you know? The real you?"

He shook his head and brought his eyes back to mine. "Nope. Not a chance. Cyrano or nothing. I can't risk my job. I need the money."

My phone buzzed, my mom's face popping up on the screen. I hit "ignore" for the third time that morning.

I continued, "Maybe you could go to another store, or maybe even—"

"I can't." He shifted in his chair. "I made my bed. Now I have to lie in it."

"I understand." I bit my lip before offering any more unwanted advice.

Besides, my personal life was in a shambles. I had no room to give anyone pointers on how to act. After the scene outside the restaurant, Mom and Carter tried to talk me into breaking it off with Braden. They didn't understand that he wasn't some one-and-done guy. I'd been through more than my fair share of those.

Braden—even though he was clumsy and ham-handed when it came to emotions—was my man. I'd known it since we first met. Some people didn't believe in love at first sight, but I did. And the moment Braden smiled at me and asked me to drinks after a game, my heart belonged to him. Neither Carter nor my mom could change that.

Just because things were rocky didn't mean we were over. The thought of Braden and I being done made me take a deep breath. I tried to push the trade and our other troubles out of my mind. If I could focus on work, maybe I wouldn't hurt so much.

"Nikki, you all right?" Cyrus cocked his head to the side.

"I'm good. Sorry. Sometimes I just zone the fuck out." Leaning forward, I poised my fingers over my keyboard. "Okay, final question. When a client asks you to—"

A ruckus in the hallway interrupted my question. A rumbling sound caught my ear, and someone was talking far too loudly in our quiet office. I cringed when I recognized the voice.

"This place is littered with hot bitches. Have I died and gone to poon-hound heaven? Hey, you in the green. I'm Kasey. What's your name, sugar?"

"Oh, my God." I stood and bolted into the hallway, but almost fell over something blocking the narrow area outside my door.

Cyrus grabbed my arm and pulled me upright before I toppled into the stack of brand new Luis Vuitton luggage.

I flailed for a moment then got my balance. "What the—"

"Nik, babe." Kasey leaned against the tallest suitcase, one that was likely worth more than my car. "You are looking mighty fine. Who's the guy?"

I stared at the luggage, unable to form words as a few other assistants crowded behind Kasey to coo over the amazing set.

Kasey glanced over her shoulder. "Come closer girls. Plenty of room for everyone." She reached behind her and drew a piece of paper from her back pocket. "From Braden."

I took the note from her.

She turned to the assistants at her back. "My work here is done. Now, I'm going to get some lunch. Who wants to blow this taco stand and go to a *specialty* taco stand, eh? Satisfaction guaranteed."

The assistants giggled as Kyrie came around the corner. "What is going on? Kasey?"

"Yeah, I was just playing delivery boy for Braden." Kasey looped her arm around one of the assistant's waist. "You look hungry, doll."

"Whitney, go on back to your desk." Kyrie frowned and pulled the assistant from Kasey's grasp.

"Cock block," Kasey muttered and kept walking toward the elevator. "I'll be down the street at Vittles and Vino for the next hour," she announced. "Whichever one of you ladies—or more than one—are welcome to join. You won't regret it. And, remember, it's not cheating if it's with a chick." Her voice faded down the hallway.

"Nik, you okay?" Kyrie scooted past the luggage, barely, and came to my side. "You've never been silent for this long in your life."

I came from a rich family, but not even my mother owned a full set of Louis Vuitton luggage. "This is too much. This is…"

"Amazing." Kyrie ran her hand along the smooth canvas with the signature monogram.

Cyrus whistled. "This is the holy grail of luggage."

"What's the note?" Kyrie pointed to the piece of paper clutched in my hand.

"From Braden. I'm just so… I can't even …" Luggage. It could only mean one thing. He wanted me to go with him if he were traded. I wanted to squeal with delight. But now that I'd had more time to think about it, I also wondered what would happen to my career if I left. What about my editor dreams? Braden was the one, but would I sacrifice my career, my *identity* to stay with him?

"And you are?" Kyrie held out her hand to Cyrus.

"Cyrus—I mean, Cyrano." He shook.

"Oh yeah. Nikki told me about you. Nice to meet you." She edged closer to me. "Not to be rude, but can I get a minute with my friend?"

"Oh, of course." Cyrus backed away. "I'll wait out here."

"Thanks." Kyrie pulled me into my office and shut the door behind us. "Open it."

My fingers didn't seem to work as I gripped the note.

"Here." She snagged it from my hands and unfolded it. "Jesus, his handwriting is atrocious. Here goes.

Nikki,

I love you. I've fucked up a lot lately. I know you know that. But I want you to know that you are the most important thing to me. I'm sorry about what happened at your parents' house. I want another chance with you and with them, even your mom. I want them to know how much I love you and that I would never, ever hurt you. Carter, though, I don't want another chance with him. I may go Easton on him if I see him touch you again. Just FYI. Okay, where was I? Right, I love you. I want you with me always. If I get traded, I want you with me. I just assumed that all schlong." Kyrie shook her head and peered closer at the paper. "It really looks like it says 'all schlong.' I'm not kidding."

I laughed and wiped away a tear. "Keep going. Is there more?"

"Yeah sorry. I think he meant 'all along' there. Anyway, it goes on: *I'm going to come clean and spill it all. I don't want to lose you*—"

"Ladies, do not touch the goods!" Cyrus' strong voice cut through Kyrie's recitation. "You can look and wish you had a man who loved you this much—I'm free tonight, by the way—but do not touch or so help me!"

Kyrie raised an eyebrow. "He's a keeper."

I sniffled. "I know. I think I have a plan for him, maybe. We'll talk later. Go on."

"I'm afraid I'm not playing ball as well as I should. My numbers are shit. I'm afraid about the trade. I don't want to leave and take you away from your work and our friends. And, this is the worst part and I really hope you won't be mad, but it's okay if you are. I hurt my knee last week. That night when I was in bed and you—" Kyrie pulled the paper away from her face as her cheeks turned red "*—sat on my face, my knee was hurt. It's still hurt. It's why I didn't move from the couch the other day, and why I didn't chase you when you walked out. I tried, but I fell and floundered around like a twat. I'm afraid to go to the doctor about it. Everything I've fucked up, I've done out of fear. But I'm not afraid as long as you're with me. You're my life. Not baseball. I'm sorry. Please forgive me. I love you."*

I sank down in my office chair. "He's hurt."

Kyrie flipped the page over. "That's it."

"He's been hurt this whole time." I rubbed my eyes, not giving a shit that I was smearing my mascara.

"You couldn't have known that." Kyrie walked behind me and wrapped her arms around my shoulders.

I leaned my head back into her soft tits and tried to figure out what the hell I was feeling. Livid, that he didn't tell me about the injury, but sad that he was so afraid of everything.

"He should have told me all of it." My tears were a given, coursing down my face as Kyrie held me.

"They do this. Bottle everything up. Easton is the same way, but worse, because of his temper. Braden wants to repair your relationship. That's the most important thing. Everything else is small stuff." She kissed the top of my head.

"And we don't sweat the small stuff."

"Right."

"I need to talk to him. We need to get his knee seen to and figure out what's going on with the trade."

"We will. I'll ask Easton—"

"Ladies, I'm not kidding. Paws off!" Cyrus sounded like a lion tamer who was about to lose control of his pussies.

"What can I do?" Kyrie straightened and walked around my desk to face me.

"I don't know." I tried to prioritize everything. "First, the doctor, then I need to solve this thing with my mom and Carter. Right?"

"Sounds like a plan." She nodded and snagged some tissues from the corner of my desk and handed them to me. "Clean yourself up. You look like you've starred in a non-consensual porn."

That drew a laugh from me as I scrubbed under my eyes. "I think my nasty sense of humor has rubbed off on you."

She smiled and pulled the collar of her sensible cardigan closed. "Certainly not. I'm a fucking lady, and don't you forget it."

I laughed and cleared away the last of my tears. "Right. Thanks."

"Anytime. You've dealt with enough of my Easton drama that I need to support you through at least five more meltdowns before we're even." She opened my door.

Cyrus was pointing a finger at someone down the hall.

"You're hot, but I'm not above hitting you to keep you off Nikki's stuff."

Kyrie laughed and shooed the assistants away as my cell rang. Mom was calling again. *Shit.* I wasn't ready for this conversation, but I wanted to clear the air sooner rather than later.

"Cyrus, can you do me one more favor and wait a little longer? I need to talk to my mom." I held up my phone.

"You got it." He swung my door closed again.

I took a deep breath and swiped across the screen. "Mom."

"Hi darling. How are you? I just wanted to make sure Braden hadn't done anything else. We could call the family lawyer if you're worried—"

"Mom—"

"—about him showing up at your work—"

"Mom!"

"What?"

"Braden and I are together. We will always be together. Nothing you say or do can change that. He's a good guy—"

"Nikki—"

"No, Mom. Let me finish. He's a good guy. He's, honestly, the best thing that's ever happened to me. When I'm with him, I'm happy. If you can't accept him, then you can't accept me. I love you and Dad, but Braden is my future. Give him another chance. Do it for me. Let him show you what sort of man he really is. No preconceptions. No Carter. Just us. Can you do that?"

She cleared her throat and stayed silent for several heavy seconds. "Nik, I think maybe you should spend some time away from him. Maybe come with us to Florida."

"Mom, I'm never going to be away from him. Do you understand? He's it for me. Either you are on board with that or you aren't. So what's it going to be?"

More silence.

I pulled the phone away from my ear, making sure we were still connected.

When I put it back, her voice came through. "I'll have to think about it. I don't trust him."

Her words were like an ice bath, but I withstood it.

"Think about it. When you're ready to talk, call me again. But be prepared to talk to the *both* of us."

She sighed with her usual dramatic flair. "I know you're stuck on him, but Carter is so—"

"Bye, Mom. Love you." I tapped the screen and ended the call.

I felt lighter, telling Mom that Braden was forever somehow lifted a weight from my shoulders. There was only one thing left to do—sit on Braden's face until we made up.

CHAPTER SIXTEEN

BRADEN

IT WAS LATE, SOMETIME around 11p.m., when I finally drove up to my apartment building. Pulling into the parking garage, I sat there for a moment and collected my thoughts. We'd won all three games during an away series in Kansas City, and while I should've been happy, all I could focus on was the pain in my knee. It was getting worse. Nikki being gone was the icing on the cake. I looked around at my fancy apartment building, and my nice car, but only one thought ran through my mind.

I've got nothing.

I opened the door of my car and hopped down on my good leg. "Fuck it." My bags could wait. I just wanted to crawl into my bed, figure out how I'd get through practice tomorrow, and how I'd make it through the upcoming home series.

I took the elevator to my floor and limped to the front door. I unlocked it and eased it open.

"Alarm activated." The computer voice rang out.

"Fucking tits. Goddamn alarm!" I hopped toward the illuminated blue screen on the wall across the entry way. My tennis shoes squeaked on the tile.

"Please enter your code."

"I heard you, cunt trap. I'm trying, fuck." I sped up on my good leg, hopping through the dark like a human pogo stick.

"Oh sh—" My leg caught on something in the way and I

face planted right in the middle of what felt like hard boxes. "Son of a motherfucker. What in the—"

The lights in the house turned on and momentarily blinded me.

I rubbed my eyes hard, trying to make out what the fuck I'd just landed in the middle of, when I saw the letters on the luggage. LV.

"Braden? Oh my God, baby. Your knee." Nik, rubbing her eyes, sprinted over in a lacy white teddy.

My heart warmed at the sight of her, and I forgot about my pain altogether.

"Are you okay?" She leaned down, and all I could do was smile and stare into her eyes, and then down at her tits, of course.

"I see you got my gift." I grinned and turned my gaze from her tits to her face. "I think I'm stuck here." I chuckled.

She giggled. "Just sit still and let me help you."

God, I'd missed her laugh. It seemed like ages since I'd heard it.

"You have five, four . . ."

"Shit, babe. Can you punch in the code? I don't want the security company showing up." I pointed at the alarm.

"Oh yeah, I got it."

I watched her run over toward the wall. Her ass jiggling in the lacy panties had my cock jutting into the expensive luggage.

You get the mushroom stamp of approval there, Louis. Apologies.

Nik hustled back over and helped me to my feet. When I was upright, she started to talk, and I put both my palms on her cheeks and my lips crashed into hers. She tried to pull away. Not a fucking chance. I raked my fingers through her hair and her lips parted, our tongues dancing back and forth across one another.

I released her and she began to speak. "Braden, we need—"

I smacked her on the ass across the panties that cut

halfway up her cheeks, and I leaned in next to her ear. "We have other business first, slut."

She let out a squeal as I kissed down her neck to her collarbone and gripped one of her breasts firm in my hand. When I tweaked her hard nipple through the soft fabric, she seized up and her breath hitched.

"God, how do you know how to touch me just right?" She ran her nails up the back of my shirt and dug them into my shoulders.

"Because we're perfect for each other." I fisted a handful of her hair and my mouth was hot in her ear as I licked slowly around it. I gripped her by the wrist and shoved her hand onto my cock. "And right now, I need you coming on my mouth, and then on my cock like a good little whore, okay?"

Her hips surged into me, and she ground her pussy up against my dick, before nodding.

I squeezed harder on her hair and a slight yelp escaped her lips. "I want you on the bed in ten seconds. Be naked when I get there."

She gripped the ass of my jeans and bit down on my earlobe before exhaling heavily in my ear. "You better hurry. I'm wet and in need of a spanking."

She turned to walk away and I smacked her hard on the ass, leaving a big red hand print.

"Oh my God." She swayed her hips as she did a little seductive runway walk toward the room, then turned and smiled before disappearing around the corner into the hallway.

Fuck!

My cock was so goddamn hard I could barely think straight. I needed it buried in her pussy five minutes ago. I planned to remedy that immediately.

Nothing in the world was better than hearing Nik tell me to fuck her like a slut while I pumped in and out of her. I stumbled toward the bedroom as fast as I could. When I turned the corner into the hallway, I thought my dick might knock some pictures off the side table.

"Lead me to the Promised Land, buddy." I gave the tent in my pants a quick glance as he led me to the room, in search of Nik's pussy. He was geared up for battle, ready to conquer and destroy.

I walked to the bedroom door and propped my arm against the frame, giving my knee a second to recover. When I looked to the bed, Nik was naked just like I'd told her. She scissored her legs together, and I realized how much I'd missed the way she looked at me.

I pulled my shirt up over my head, and a tingling rushed across my exposed skin. The heat from Nikki's stare sent blood rushing into my cock as I pulled my shoes off. I unbuttoned my jeans and yanked them to my ankles.

When I took my briefs down and let my cock spring out from captivity, Nik licked her lips and spread her legs.

"That's a good girl. I haven't had a proper meal in a while."

Her head flew back against the sheets. "Fuck, you have the dirtiest mouth. It does things to me, Braden."

I eyed her like a wolf after its prey, stalking toward the bed. I hovered over her, roving every inch of her gorgeous body with my eyes before gripping her hard at the waist. "I know." I smirked.

Flipping her over to her stomach, I jerked her petite frame to the edge so that she was bent over the bed, and I smacked her ass once more. I leaned next to her head and my cock pressed against the edges of her slippery folds. "You are wet, aren't you?"

"Mmhmm," she cooed.

I grabbed her gently around the throat, just enough to turn her head to me, and smashed my lips against hers, before forcing her to open up, so I could feel her tongue on mine once more. We broke our kiss after a long moment, and I whispered, "You're going to come on my face, and then on my dick. Got me, slut?" I squeezed her throat a tiny bit and her eyes rolled back before returning to me.

"Please." She dropped her face into the sheets as I released my hold on her.

I lowered and shifted all of my weight onto my good knee on the floor, and began to massage her ass cheeks in my hands before spreading them apart. "Look at this pink, wet pussy. Mmm. Wonder what would happen if I licked on it?"

Her legs quivered at my words. I slid my fingers down her thighs and her muscles tightened. Kissing up the soft skin on the insides of her legs, I ran my tongue all the way up to her clit, and then flattened my tongue on her pussy and licked back the entire length.

Nikki gasped, and her legs shuddered once more. "I missed this slutty little cunt of yours."

"God." Her voice was a breathy exhale.

I stroked my tongue around her lips, spreading her ass hard with my hands, and then flicked my tongue on her clit. I wrapped my lips around it and sucked, hard. Her hips jolted forward, and she started to grind her ass up and down on my face.

Tasting her pussy, knowing what my tongue could do to her, had my cock harder than all the diamonds in Easton's browser history. I fought the urge to stand up and fuck her senseless. I'd promised her she'd come on my face, after all.

I worked her clit with my tongue, increasing the tempo until I could feel the orgasm about to rip through her body. I dug my nails into her ass and pinned her against the bed. The sheets flew up toward her face, which meant she must have yanked them up to her. I held her still and shook my head furiously against her hot entrance, darting my tongue back and forth across her pussy and her clit.

"Fuck, Braden." She trembled under my touch as she stiffened and moaned, coming all over my face, as I lashed across her with my tongue. After a brief second, she finally relaxed against the bed and I rose to my feet.

She started to lean up and I splayed my fingers across her back and shoved her down into the bed. "Stay. It's time for part two of my promise."

I smacked her across the ass with my free hand and then fisted my cock and shoved it inside of her. It'd been awhile since I'd buried myself in Nikki. Too fucking long. Her warm pussy hugged tight around my cock, and I could feel her squeezing her slippery walls on me. She squealed as I leaned over her back, keeping as much weight on my good leg as possible while my chest pressed up against her. I pushed inside as far as I could, and her breathing sped up against the sheets.

"I don't think you've ever made me this hard before. You like it deep, slut?" I pushed even farther inside of her, smashing my hips into her ass.

"Jesus, I'm about to come already." Her words were barely more than a whisper.

I moved my bad knee up onto the bed and repositioned myself. One hand reached over her back and clamped down on her shoulder, the other gripped hard on the side of her hip as I tried to pull her back into me and bury my cock deeper.

She belted out a moan. "Fuck."

"If you say so." I pulled out nearly to the tip and then rammed back into her, hard, jolting her against the bed.

Her scream echoed off the wall, before she buried her face into the sheets, muffling the sound. My hand that was on her hip spanked her again, and I thrust into her once more. "You like that, slut? Tell me."

"God, you know I love it when you fuck me like a dirty slut."

My balls tightened up at her words. She loved dirty talk, and so did I. I didn't know how much longer I could possibly last inside of her. It was time to do work.

"You might want to hold on for this."

She turned her head and attempted to glance back at me when I started yanking her hips into me as I pounded forward. The sound of wet skin slapping together rang through the room before being engulfed by her screams. I pumped into her as fast as I could, each thrust trying to pull her into me harder.

I slid my hand from her shoulder up into her hair and wrapped the strands around my hand before yanking her head up so that she was staring straight ahead. My cock pistoned into her until I couldn't stop my load from working up my shaft.

"Come on my dick like a good little slut." I gave her another slap on the ass and dug my fingers into her soft, tanned skin.

"Oh my—" Her pussy clamped down on me, and it was all over. I shoved as far in as I could and shot deep inside of her. Her pussy walls spasmed around me, trying to milk every last drop from my dick.

Fuzzy stars formed in my vision as I thrust one last time before collapsing onto her back, my semi-hard cock still halfway lodged inside.

I brushed a few sweaty strands of blonde hair from her back and kissed around her shoulder blades and up to her nape. "God, that was fucking hot."

"Mmhmm." She nodded with her eyes closed, a huge grin spread across her face.

After taking a moment to recover, I let it out. "I'm sorry. I shouldn't have hid things from you. We're a team. I was wrong to do that."

I pulled my cock out of Nikki and fell next to her on the bed. She opened her eyes and put a palm on my cheek. "I'm sorry about my family. I've told them a hundred times that you and I are in it for the long haul. I thought things were turning around with Mom, and then she ambushed me at the restaurant with Carter again. I left. That's why I was outside."

"I haven't exactly made it easy for your family to like me. I'm trying to work on it. I promise." I scrubbed a hand across my sweaty face. "*We* will figure it out. I'm still getting used to my life not being a one man show. But, I don't know who I am without you around anymore. And the knee thing isn't helping."

"You need to see a doctor." Nik glared at me.

"It's not that simple, babe. An injury guarantees I'll be traded. I have to play." I stared hard at her for another moment. "I have to."

Her look of concern made me love her even more. She cared about me. I got it. But, I couldn't be traded. I didn't want her to choose between me and her career. Mostly, I was afraid of what the doctor might say. I couldn't handle the truth about my knee right now. What if it was a major injury? What if my career was over? What if he told me I couldn't play baseball anymore?

"You can hardly walk when you're *not* playing through the pain. It's not going to heal. You might be making it worse." She lifted my chin with a finger. "But, I'll back whatever you do, babe. You know this. Just don't hide it from me. Please."

I leaned over and kissed her on the forehead. "I won't hide anything else from you ever again. I promise."

CHAPTER SEVENTEEN
NIKKI

"BATTER, BATTER, BATTER! FEEL that dick in your ass? It's mine, and I'm about to blow!" I yelled as Easton whipped his arm around and let loose with a blistering fastball.

The batter swung after the ball smacked safely into Braden's glove. Strike out. The crowd roared as the inning ended and the teams switched positions. Night had fallen, and the stadium lights hummed high overhead.

"Ha!" I sank into my seat and Kasey handed me the popcorn. "That was all me."

"You struck out the last three hitters?" Kyrie raised an eyebrow and took a handful of popcorn. "I thought that was my boyfriend out there on the mound."

"I mean, sure Easton was actually throwing the ball and stuff, but I was the one who distracted the guys at bat."

"Keep telling yourself that." She popped a single piece of popcorn into her mouth while I dumped a handful into mine.

"No wonder Braden loves you. If you can put that much popcorn in your mouth—" Kasey winced "—Yick, I just thought about dick in your mouth. Not cool." She snugged her baseball cap lower on her forehead. "Pussy, pussy, only pussy, if you suck a dick, you deserve it in your tushy."

"Is that a mantra?" I crunched through the popcorn as the relief pitcher for the Marlins threw a few warmup pitches.

135

"Words to live by." Kasey smiled and took a gulp of beer.

"I read your article on Cyrano this morning, by the way." Kyrie brushed some stray kernels off her Easton Holliday jersey. "I loved it."

"Loved it?" I couldn't hold back my grin.

"No doubt. It's your best work yet. I may have even set up a meeting with Graciela about you—"

I gasped. "Really?" Was she going to push for me to move up to an editor spot?

"But don't get your hopes up." She squeezed my arm. "It's tough to make the leap. It may take more time and articles from you, but I want to broach the subject sooner rather than later and take her temperature."

Excitement welled inside me and I grabbed Kyrie in a messy, popcorn-y embrace. "Thank you!"

"This is more like it." Kasey pressed herself against my back and reached around to catch both Kyrie and me in her arms.

"You're welcome." Kyrie squeezed me a little tighter. "I'll let you know what comes of it."

"I love being just one of the girls." Kasey nuzzled into my hair.

"Perv." I elbowed Kasey away and settled back into my seat.

Kasey frowned, but then her expression lightened. "Say, Nik, you never gave me all the details from the lez experience you had in college. This game is boring as fuck. Entertain me with it."

"It wasn't really an experience. I just kissed a girl a little bit when I was drunk." I shrugged as the first Ravens batter, Ramirez, strode to the plate.

"Not bad." Kasey crossed her long, tan legs at the knee.

The guy sitting next to her gave her an appreciative up and down look, but her head was turned towards me so she didn't see it.

"How much tongue are we talking?"

I closed my eyes and tried to remember the fall of my sophomore year, but it was hazy at best. I had way too much fun in school. "I think there was tongue, and she definitely felt me up over my shirt. I can't remember if she ever went under, but I doubt it."

"Nice." Kasey set her beer down. "I think I need a reenactment. You know, to test you. Make sure you're not running a game on Braden, *pretending* to be straight."

I rolled my eyes as Ramirez swung and missed, strike one. "Not a chance. Besides, everyone knows I'm a Penis Flytrap."

"Come on, just a little kiss." She leaned closer as Kyrie snickered on my other side.

"No way." I shook my head. "Braden would kill me."

"I think Braden would be all about it. Just a couple of girls. One, his girlfriend, the other, like a sister to him. No harm in the two of us being friendly. Right, Kyrie?"

"Don't drag me into this. I'm an innocent bystander." She grabbed some more popcorn as Kasey's confident grin surfaced.

I tried to ignore the hot blonde trying to get into my panties. The next pitch was high and outside. Ball.

"Just a little experiment. That's all." Kasey's tone turned wheedling. "It won't count."

"How many girls have you tricked into opening their legs for you like this?" I stared at her, not even close to falling under her spell.

She frowned. "Tons. What gives with you?"

"I love Braden."

"Me too." She moved closer, her big, pretty eyes open wide like the wolf's in Red Riding Hood. "So how about you give me a little tit action as a sign of our love for him."

Kyrie snorted.

"A little help here?" I turned to her.

"Nope." She shook her head, a giggle falling from her lips. "I don't get between Kasey and her prey."

"Come on." Kasey wrapped a lock of my hair around her

finger.

I tried to keep the amused smile off my lips. "I'm trying to watch the game."

Ramirez finally made contact, hitting a line drive and trucking it to first base.

Kasey didn't even look. She kept her gaze on me.

I sighed. "Oh my God. If I say yes, will you leave me alone?"

She squealed. "Yes, I promise."

"Fine, you can have a tit grope." I'd taken many a tit grope from Kyrie, so this was nothing special.

She reached for the hem of my tank top.

"Hey!" I smacked her hand away. "*Over* my shirt and for no more than five seconds."

"That's it?" she pouted.

I tossed my hair behind my shoulder. "It's that or nothing, you goddamn sexual predator."

She smiled and licked her lips before focusing on my chest. "Fine."

"Get to it." I leaned back and dropped my elbows to the armrest, giving her maximum chest exposure.

She rubbed her hands together like she was Mr. Miyagi readying to fix Daniel-San's leg. The guy sitting on her other side couldn't take his eyes off us. I wondered if he was going to cream in his jeans.

"Here we go." She hovered her hands over my chest as Kyrie shook with laughter next to me. "Luscious Nikki tits in three, two, one."

"Hey!" Braden's voice cut through the air.

I looked up and Kasey and I were on the kiss cam for the entire stadium to see.

"Kase!" I leaned forward, but that only pressed her palms to my tits.

The crowd went silent, and Kasey took the opportunity to give me a good squeeze. I smacked her hands away as the crowd went from silent to roaring with approval. I hid my scarlet face in my hands.

"Goddammit Kasey!" Braden was at the net yelling. "I'm going to kick your ass!"

I peeked through my fingers as a grinning Easton strode up behind him. "Come on, man. They're just dicking around."

"Kasey is a woman-stealer. She's the devil!" He pointed a finger through the netting at Kasey, who was doubled over with laughter.

"I'm sorry." I shook my head, my hands still covering my face.

"It's not your fault. It's the blonde Satan sitting next to you!" The corner of his mouth twitched. He was holding back a smile.

"You boys going to play ball or what?" The umpire walked up behind Easton.

"We are." Easton pulled Braden away from the net and forced him to turn back toward the field. He shot Kasey a hard look. "Lay off, dick. We're trying to do work out here."

"My bad." Kasey sat up and wiped the tears from under her eyes. "But Jeez, bro, they are just so soft, yet firm!"

Braden tried to turn, but Easton kept him moving toward home plate.

"Sorry!" I called again.

Braden looked over his shoulder, pointed two fingers at his eyes and the same fingers at Kasey. She chuckled as he took his bat from the batboy and did a few practice swings. After one more glare at Kasey, he stepped into the batter's box.

The embarrassment of being felt up on the kiss-cam faded, and worry took its place. My stomach churned at the thought of Braden having to run full-speed to first base. He'd been covering his limp for the entire game, but I knew he was in pain.

"Maybe you should have waited to pull your devilry until after Braden's turn at-bat." Kyrie slurped her Icee.

"Don't go pretending like I haven't gotten a handful of *your* lovely lady lumps." Kasey wore a self-satisfied grin before downing the rest of her beer.

"What?" I gaped at Kyrie. "Why'd you let her get me, too?"

She shrugged. "I thought maybe you'd have a chance of staying strong."

"Against *my* lezzy wiles? Pfft. Give me a break." Kasey stood. "I've got to take a leak. You girls try and keep it classy while I'm gone."

Everything else faded as I focused on Braden and prayed his knee injury wouldn't affect anything during his at-bat. A walk would be the best outcome, but not likely. His numbers weren't great, and the pitcher would try and take full advantage of that fact. I didn't want him to strike out, but running to first base could have been even more treacherous for him.

I perched on the edge of my seat as the pitcher came set. The first pitch was outside and low. Ball. The second pitch was the same. Ball. Small tendrils of relief swirled inside me with each call.

My fingers wrestled with each other as the third pitch came screaming down the middle. Strike.

Braden stood straight and knocked the bat against his shoes before taking position again. Another pitch, this one high and inside. Ball. He hadn't swung the bat once.

"How's his knee?" Kyrie's whisper barely made it to my ear.

"I don't know. Not good." I kept my voice low as the next pitch slapped into the catcher's glove. Strike.

The count was full. The next pitch would result in a walk, a strike-out, or a hit. The crowd quieted as Braden stepped to the plate again.

I held my breath as the pitcher came set. His powerful leg kick seemed to happen in slow motion. The ball hurtled toward home plate, and Braden swung.

The crack of the bat had me searching the sky for the ball. It flew out over the short stop's head. I dragged my gaze back to Braden who had taken off for first base. He came down heavy on his uninjured leg, his stride uneven.

Kyrie took my hand and squeezed it.

"Can you tell?" I winced as he continued his awkward gait.

The ball dropped in left field and was quickly scooped up by an outfielder who tossed it in to second base. Braden barely rounded first at all and quickly took a few steps back to the base. He'd gotten a single, but I prayed that management hadn't been able to tell he was injured.

Kyrie hadn't answered my question.

I squeezed her hand. "Tell me. Did you see it?"

She withdrew her hand and threw her arm around my shoulder, pulling me in close. "Yeah. I could tell. I'm sorry."

My fingers went cold and I felt the blood drain from my face. If Kyrie could see it, that meant everyone else—including the team management—could, too.

CHAPTER EIGHTEEN
BRADEN

I STOOD ON FIRST base, and the throb in my knee was constant. I knew I'd done more damage running out that base hit. *Fuck*.

"Braden!"

I caught Coach's glare in the corner of my eye. He leaned over the railing separating the dugout from the field. His eyes were sharp and insistent. I quickly shook my head in his direction, trying not to draw any added attention from people in the front office who may have been watching. Coach shoved off the rail and stalked back and forth in the dugout.

As the pitcher came set, I took my lead from first. My eyes were trained on his feet. I was pretty sure everyone in the stadium had seen me hobble, but I pretended nothing was wrong. The pitcher flashed me a grin and spun quickly with a pick off move.

When I pushed off on my leg, I let out an audible groan before I dove back into the bag and barely beat the tag. My jaw clenched, and I grunted under my breath. I rose back to my feet and brushed the dirt from the front of my jersey.

The first baseman tossed the ball back to the pitcher, and the pitcher took to the mound once more. This time I barely took a lead at all, remaining close enough to first that I wouldn't have to dive back. The pitcher came set before kicking his leg and firing a fastball. Crack.

A sharp groundball screamed toward the second

baseman, and he quickly tossed it to the shortstop as Ramirez sprinted toward home. I froze in the base path. They had turned a double play, but Ramirez trotted across home plate scoring another run for us. I walked back to the dugout barely able to hide my limp.

Once I was down the stairs, Coach was up in my face. "You're not going back out there."

"Bullshit." I tried to move past him and his large hand whacked me in the chest.

"You're done until you see a doctor." His brows pinched together, and he scowled, but I could sense concern in his eyes.

I dropped my head and stared at the ground for a quick second before looking back up at him. "I can't come out of the game. You know I can't."

"Son—" he placed a hand on my shoulder, "—you can't play like this. I'm sorry. You're not fooling anyone up there anymore." He lifted his head back toward the skybox where all the rich fucks sat to watch the game. "Trust me. They know."

I wanted to break down, but I couldn't let the guys see me defeated. "Okay."

Coach leaned up next to my ear. "There are more ways to be a leader than being on the field. I'll figure out something to tell Ingram. Maybe I can buy us some time. But you need to see a doctor tomorrow. Until then, you're not going out on that field."

"Whatever is best for the team." I turned to walk away, and his fingers dug into my forearm.

"You're sick. If you see Ingram, walk straight and fake it the best you can. Got me?"

I grinned and gave a dramatic shiver. "I do feel a bit feverish."

"I thought so." His voice rose to where the other guys could hear him. "Probably need some antibiotics or something. There's a bug going around. The guys will pick you up though."

I stared around at my teammates. They all knew the score and had grins on their faces. Ramirez walked up to Coach and me. "You know, Coach. My grandma makes this little drink with whiskey and stuff. It'll cure anything. You can put like dandelions, mint leaves," he paused, "a little cannabis in that shit. It makes you just right as all hell the next day." He chuckled at both of us.

"Jesus Christ, when are we trading you?" Coach chortled and walked away.

Ramirez spun around to face Coach's back and held his arms out wide. "Well goddamn, man. I'm just trying to help around here. A little weed never hurt anybody. Shit."

The other guys grabbed their mitts as our hitter grounded out to third. Ramirez leaned up by my ear. "I'm new around here, but I know respect when I see it. These fellas got your back. I do too, *Captain.*"

His words resonated with me. I struggled to walk to the end of the dugout where my replacement was strapping on his gear. The kid was a rookie. His fingers shook as he reached for his glove. He'd played a few games, but we were usually up eight runs or so any time he saw the field.

When I walked up, he dropped his glove. I could see the fear on his face and sensed it in his movements. It was the same fear I'd had when I started my first big league game. It was important that I make him comfortable. He was in charge now, and the team needed him. Giving him confidence was paramount, and I couldn't help him if I moped around, worried about my own problems.

"Hey, you've done this a thousand times. Okay?"

He nodded and pulled the chest protector over his head. He started to hook it around his waist when I grabbed the strap at his neck and yanked him over to me, mainly because my leg hurt too much to stand up and get in his face.

"Are you scared?" I glared at him. He was clearly scared shitless, and I had a responsibility to make sure he didn't fuck up. "Be honest with me."

"Y-yeah. I am."

145

"Get over it. You're in charge out there." I pulled him in closer, so that he was inches from my face. "That's your motherfucking field out there. You wear the gear. You're in charge. Your attitude reflects on those guys. If you're scared, they're scared. Now walk out on the field like you're a fucking all-star and command your fucking troops. Got me?"

Something changed in his eyes. He straightened up and stuck his chest out. "Yes, sir."

"Good." I'd done the hard-ass bit, and now I needed to reassure him. "The fact you have that uniform on means you're good enough to be here. You're as good as me. Play smart. Be yourself. Play *your* game."

"I will. I promise, B."

"Good."

He turned to take the field.

"Hey, kid?"

His head whipped back around to me. "Yeah?"

"I'm right here, man. I'm not going anywhere. You've got *their* back." I glanced out to the field. "And I've got *yours*." I held out my fist and he tapped it with his catcher's mitt. "Go kick some ass and take my job."

It was the worst advice I could've given him for me personally, but it was best for the team. That was the kind of thing that'd earned me respect with the guys over the years, and I wanted to instill that same thing into the rook.

I smacked the rookie on the ass as he strutted into the clubhouse. The kid hit a walk off double in the bottom of the ninth to win the game. It was huge, and I couldn't have been more fucking proud of him as he showed me a sheepish grin.

"Thanks for helping me with my nerves. I don't think I

would've played that well if it hadn't been for our little talk."

On the inside, I could already feel myself being pushed out of my position. The kid was damn good. He was young, and inexperienced, but he had talent in spades. "Bullshit, rook. That was all you." I pounded a finger into his chest. "*You* did that, not me."

"All the same. You're still the Cap." He gave me a nod. It was the gesture players used to show respect to one another. "Thanks."

"You just wait until my kn—" I stopped myself and cleared my throat as Ingram stalked past us in the clubhouse. He glared at me. "Wait until this stomach bug passes. You're going to have to fight for that spot."

Rook started to say something else when I heard a crack, and his eyes shot wide open. "Holy shit!" He winced and reached back for his ass when I heard a familiar cackle.

"Atta boy, rook! Nice rip out there." Easton had lit him up with a hard slap to the ass. It was his trademark celebratory gesture that often left people unable to sit for a week.

I couldn't contain my laughter as the rookie walked away with the quickness. "Damn, that shit sounded brutal."

"Yeah, my hand kind of stings a bit. Got that ass good." Easton shook his hand out to the side. "I saw Ingram walk into Coach's office. It won't be pretty."

"Coach is going to tell him I have the flu. Try and hold him over until I can see the doctor." I stripped off my jersey and tossed it into the big hamper by the lockers. The musty smell would be enough to send most people running for the door, but we were all used to it. I'd miss it if I had to hang up my cleats for good.

"Good. Maybe he'll buy it."

"Not a chance, man. I'm so fucked. Doc is going to say I need surgery. It's been weeks and it's getting worse. If it's my ACL, I'm fucking done."

"Maybe if you'd gone earlier, like smart people told your dumb ass to do, you wouldn't be in this predicament." He sat down on the bench in the middle of the room. I sat on the other side, facing the other direction and dropped my head into my hands.

He bent over and started to untie one of his shoes. "I'm sorry. I shouldn't have said that. I know what has to be going through your mind right now. Just stop assuming the worst-case scenario. Knees are funny. You know this."

"I know, but there's a lot riding on whatever the doctor says. I could be released or traded." I scrubbed my hands up and down my cheeks. "I know Nik will go with me if I'm traded. But she's excited and doing well at her job. I can't ask her to leave everything. And what will I do? Baseball is all I know." I turned back to Easton.

"Don't think like that." He sighed. It was the hardest thing for a baseball player to talk about — when their playing days were over. "I don't know what I'll do without you if it's serious. Wish the front office could see more than numbers. You make everyone so much better out there. You make me better. It's a tough situation."

I looked down and saw the whites in his knuckles from the grip he had on the bench.

"I don't know what to tell you, man. Nik loves you. She'll go with you. I don't doubt that for a second. I wish I had better advice to give. The whole situation sucks a fat-ass dick."

Hollers rang out from Coach's office. It wasn't uncommon when he and Ingram were left alone together.

"The flu my ass. You are so full of shit." Ingram burst through the door and stalked through the clubhouse, glaring at Easton and me. He had no respect for the game. He'd never played it. Now, he'd aired my shit out for the whole clubhouse to hear.

It's not like the other guys didn't know the score, but it wasn't something that was usually done, out of respect.

My jaw clenched, and I fought the urge to beat the arrogance out of him. Easton must have sensed my frustration. His giant hand gripped my bicep, and he flashed

Ingram a big 'fuck you' smile. After Ingram was out of earshot, Easton started the conversation back up. "That guy is such a cock monkey. I'd love to get him one on one somewhere and knock some sense into him."

"Indeed, man." I attempted to straighten out my bad leg and winced. Knees were a catcher's worst nightmare, and I knew the day would come eventually. All I could do was hope for the best. I exhaled a large breath and a surprising calm came over me. I had nothing to feel guilty about now that Nik knew everything, and there were no secrets between us. We'd figure it out. No matter what, she'd be by my side. In that moment, I realized I'd finally found something more important than baseball. Something that could last forever.

I opened the front door to my apartment, and Nik lounged on the couch watching television. Her eyes lit up when they met mine, and I could tell she was trying to tamp down her excitement about something. It must have been something to do with her job — either that or her mom had called offering a full apology and an all-expenses-paid vacation. Not likely on the mom front.

She grabbed the remote and clicked off the TV.

"What's up, babe?" I hobbled over to the table, wincing with each step. My keys clanked together when I dropped them on top of the hard wood.

"Nothing. Nothing at all. How'd it go with Coach and the—" She stared at my knee.

I had the feeling she was holding back her good news, but I wanted to hear about the awesome things happening in her career. If it helped take my mind off baseball for even a second, it was worth it. I wanted to be happy for her, because she was amazing and didn't deserve my shit bringing her down.

"I want to hear your news first. You're excited about something. Tell me what it is."

"It's nothing, really." Her hands were trembling, and I could sense how hard it was for her to keep from exploding with her good news. I wasn't about to ruin it for her.

"Woman, tell me. Do I have to put my head between your legs to get the secret from you? I mean, I'm willing to make that sacrifice, if I must." I wiped my hand across my mouth and grinned.

"Mmm, a ride on your tongue does sound mighty fun. I'm not going to lie. Okay, I'll tell you." Excitement bubbled from her as she clapped her hands. I loved watching her smile at me. I wanted to see it every day for the rest of my life.

She finally calmed herself enough to speak. "So, Kyrie loved my piece. And she's going to show it to Graciela! Eek!"

"What? That's amazing, babe. The one with the Cyrano guy?" I sat up straight and did my best deep-voice impression of Cerrano from Major League. "It is very bad to steal Jobu's rum." I leaned in toward her. "It is *very* bad."

"Huh?" She stared at me the same way I looked at her when she told me about designer hand bags.

"Major League? You've never seen it?" I returned her puzzled gaze.

"Not a clue."

"First of all, that's a fucking travesty that needs to be remedied. But for right now, tell me more. I want to hear everything. What else did Kyrie say?" I pulled her into my side and she nuzzled into my chest.

"Well, if it goes well—" She popped back up on the couch. Her smile was electric, and I couldn't help but grin. "—and I'm not saying it will. But, I could be on track to making editor. At freaking *Style and Substance*!"

The radiant look on her face had my stomach churning so bad I thought I might really have the flu. I tried my best to be as happy as she was, but remembered that honesty was what we were aiming for these days. I looked down at the floor, wishing circumstances were different.

"Braden? What is it?" It was her concerned voice that I usually tried to avoid. "It's your knee, isn't it?"

I wanted my knee to be healthy. I wanted to scoop her up and carry her off to the bedroom, fuck her silly, and then take her out to celebrate her accomplishment. Why now? Why was there always something that fucked everything up?

"I want to be happy for you. Scratch that. I *am* happy for you. That's just fucking amazing, Nik, and I am so proud of you. More than you know. You're making your dreams come true. But I'm trying to be honest. Because that's kind of our thing now. Things don't look so great for me. Coach wants me to see the doctor tomorrow."

Nik fell back into the cushions of the couch. "Well, you *do* need to see one."

"I know. I'm scared of what he'll say. What if he tells me I can't play anymore?" My eyes started to water. I didn't cry often, and lately I'd been a total pussy on that front. But it was baseball. It had been my life for so long. Nik was my future, but admitting my dream was coming to an end wouldn't be easy. I took her palm in my hand and pressed it to my face. "What if he tells me I'm done?"

The look on her face crushed my soul. I hated myself for dropping all of this on her during one of the most exciting times in her life.

"Let's just wait and see what the doctor says. We'll figure it out. We're a team, you and me."

Her words made sense, but they didn't match her expression. I'd sucked all the life out of her. I couldn't handle the fleeting thought that she might change her mind about coming with me if I got traded. Anxiety coursed through my veins and settled in my stomach. It was all so much easier when I kept the shit to myself and let people enjoy themselves without worrying about my problems.

"Okay. Let's wait and see." I fell back into the couch and she rested her head on my shoulder. The decision I'd have to make was becoming clear. I knew I'd have to choose between Nik and baseball. I told myself I'd choose Nik, no matter what. But was I lying to myself?

CHAPTER NINETEEN
NIKKI

MY COMPUTER WAS BROKEN. Had to be. I kept looking at the time showing in the bottom right corner and the number didn't seem to change. I thwacked the side of the monitor with my palm and the number clicked over. Clearly, my efforts had worked.

Kyrie had been in Graciela's office for over an hour. Not that I was counting or anything. I thwacked the monitor again, but the digits mocked me and remained the same. I put my head on my desk as the familiar squeak of the mail cart filled the hallway. *Squeak … squeak … squeak.*

The sound stopped, and I could sense Grady-the-mouth-breather outside my door.

"What do you want?" I glanced up, and he was staring as usual. Couldn't he tell this was a majorly important day for me?

"I, uh, there's mail." He smiled, his comically large front teeth on display.

"Put it on my desk." I put my head back down as Grady shuffled into the room. The sound of mail flopping into my tray was followed with heavy silence. He was still in my office, but I refused to look at him again. Maybe if I kept my head down, he'd go away.

After a few more moments, I heard the distinctive *shick* of scissors. That got me to raise my head. Grady backed away with one hand hidden behind him.

I narrowed my eyes. "What did you do?"

153

"Just delivered the mail." He backed all the way out my door and returned to his cart. He kept hiding his hand, so I knew he must have had something in it.

Squeak … Squeak… The sound stopped, and I heard Grady take in a huge sniffing breath through his nose followed by a relieved-sounding "aahhh" on the exhale.

"What in the ever loving fuck?" I sat up and nearly lost my shit when I realized a few strands of my hair stayed on the desk. They'd been neatly cut. Yanking my hair out to inspect the ends, I realized Grady had cut a lock of my hair from one side. A *big* lock of hair.

I rose from my desk and darted around toward my door, not sure what I was going to do, but certain I would make it hurt.

"Grady, you fucking duckbill pervypus!" I ran into the hallway after him, but instead of Grady, Graciela was walking toward me, one eyebrow raised in displeasure.

My heart sank through the carpet and into a shredder on a lower floor. *Fuck!*

"Duckbill pervypus?" She strode past me with an air of impatience.

"I—that was—" I followed her into my office. "—we were just."

"Sit down, Nikki. It's time we had a chat." Her tone brooked no nonsense, so I closed the door and sank into my desk chair. It was probably a good thing. My knees were already wobbling.

"What can I, um, do for you Graciela?" I noticed she had a thin stack of papers in her hand.

She perched on my visitor's bench like a graceful, if bony, bird. "That's a good question." She flipped past the first page and read aloud. "*Cyrano reveals that the passion for fringe was short-lived and is already on its way out. Customers are far more interested in the faux fur revolution for the upcoming winter season.*" She laid the papers in her lap and tapped her chin. "What gave you the idea for this article?"

I pulled at the peter pan collar of my top. "Well, I was

shopping with my mother. Cyrano was helping me, and I noticed that he had a thing for tits, and as—I mean, I noticed he was straight, but he also had a killer sense of style. So, I sort of …" I took a deep breath and tried to choose the right words. "I sort of told him that he should do the story because he could get more commissions from readers who might choose him to assist them, and if he did it, I wouldn't tell people he was a straight guy named Cyrus." I delivered the last part like a question.

"So you sniffed out a story and then strong-armed the subject into cooperating?" She crossed her lean arms over her chest.

"That's putting it kind of harshly." I did my best to brush off my devious tactics. "I just sort of found a way for both of us to get what we wanted. I got a great story. He got a chance at more commissions. No harm done."

"Hmm. Let's set that aside for the moment." She leaned forward. "Are you aware that we've gotten excellent feedback about your waxing piece? It seems a lot of our readers didn't realize their salons weren't using the correct techniques or materials. We've also had several readers express gratitude to you for laying it all out in your down-to-earth style."

"I didn't know—"

She continued as if I hadn't spoken. "I confess, I didn't think you had what it took to fit in here. You're brash, and you have the filthiest mouth I've ever heard, and I used to date a Navy man." Her eyes narrowed. "But the readers are reacting to you. And this piece." She held up her hand. "I can already feel that it's going to strike a chord with our readers. It appeals to people like Cyrus, who love fashion but can't exactly afford the luxuries in the store where he works, but also appeals to the women who read our magazines while lying on the beach in the Hamptons."

My heart expanded with each of her words until I worried it might burst.

"Here's what we're going to do." She rose, her voice

authoritative. "You are promoted to the position of editor—"

I squealed, but she held up a hand.

"*Provisionally*, for six months. If, during that six months, you've continued to produce top notch work, you will be an editor, free and clear. The only reason you're getting the promotion now is so you can focus on your writing. It's hard to do that and be an assistant, as well." She smiled as much as her Botox allowed. "After all, I started as an assistant, so I know what it's like." Walking to my door, she turned. "But, mark my words, if you slack off or disappoint me, you'll be right back in this shoebox, dealing with the ad department, and getting everyone's lunch. Got me?"

I couldn't even process the words coming from her mouth, but I stuttered out a response. "Yes, I will—I mean I won't disappoint you. Thank you, Graciela." I wanted to squeeze her, but that might have turned her into a pile of vampire dust, so I just sat dumbfounded as she disappeared into the hall.

"What happened to your hair?" Kyrie walked in, the smile on her face warring with a quizzical expression.

I jumped up and ran to her. "Give me some sweet tit lovin', bestie!"

She laughed and let me snuggle against her as she plucked at the ravaged strands of hair. "But seriously, why did you do this?"

I pulled away. "You got me promoted!"

She shook her head and kept picking at my hair. "*You* got you promoted. Graciela was more than a little impressed with your Cyrano piece. It didn't hurt that I said you were capable of that on a monthly basis, on top of editing duties."

I couldn't wipe the smile off my face. "This is huge."

Kyrie snorted. "That's what she said. Now, what's with the hair?"

"Grady."

She seemed to cough on her own spit before reining it in. "You let Grady cut your hair?"

I took the few steps back to my chair and collapsed into it, my mind reeling from the news. "He cut it when I wasn't looking."

"How on earth did he manage to cut your hair without you seeing him?"

"I don't know. I had my head on my desk, and I don't even care anymore." I pinched my arm. It was real. "I'm an editor."

She nodded and leaned against my door frame. "Graciela is having the office next to mine cleared. We'll be neighbors. You'll need to hire an assistant, too."

"My own assistant?" I kicked my feet.

"*Our* assistant. We'll have to share."

"I don't care. Besides, I already know who would be perfect for it."

"Yeah?"

"Cyrus. He's all about fashion, and he guarded my luggage with his life."

She cocked her head to the side. "You're right. He's perfect. Tell him to call HR, and they'll get him all set up."

"I will. Once I come down. Right now I'm just so intensely frickin—"

"Overwhelmed? I know. Congratulations, Nik. You deserve it. I'll go and let you make some phone calls. I'm sure you're dying to tell Braden and your mom."

My sails deflated a bit. "Braden. We're going to the doctor today. If it's bad—"

She held up a hand. "It won't be. And if it is, we'll deal."

I picked at the hem of my skirt. "If he gets traded, I'll have to leave this. Even though it's finally happening for me, I'll have to give it up." I shook my head. I should have been worrying about Braden instead of myself.

"Wait and see what the doctor says before you start packing, okay?" She pointed to my phone. "Call Braden. He'll be thrilled. Trust me. Just don't tell him about Grady." She laughed. "He wouldn't like it, and I still don't know how you let that creeper cut your hair without you noticing."

When she turned to leave, I burst out laughing. She was missing a sizeable chunk of her brown hair on the left side.

"What?" She looked over her shoulder.

"Oh, nothing." I picked up the phone to call Braden. "Nothing at all."

"Is this the part where you have to give a jizz sample?" I slid between Braden's knees as he sat on the exam table, his legs dangling off the sides.

I only got a strained smile out of him. I tried again. "I hear there's a nurse here who has a strict three-finger method. How well would you say you know the limits of your own prostate?"

His smile grew bigger, and he gripped my ass, pulling me closer. "Just because I'm in a hospital gown doesn't mean I can't make you do unspeakable things until the doctor gets here." He slapped my ass.

Color rushed into my cheeks — both sets — and I got onto my tiptoes. He leaned forward and gave me a brief kiss, not the breathtaking sort I was used to. I could feel the worry rolling off him, and my attempts at distraction weren't going as well as I'd hoped.

"Oh, hang on." I turned my back to him. "I brought you something to look at while we wait."

I grabbed the latest *Style and Substance* issue from my purse and, *whoops*, dropped it on the floor. With a sly smile, I looked over my shoulder as I widened my stance and bent at the waist to retrieve it. Braden's gaze went right to my hemline, already cut to inappropriate heights, as I reached for the magazine.

He made a small strangled sound when my hands went flat on the floor. Once I had the issue in my fingers, I straightened and turned back to him as if nothing were amiss.

He swallowed hard and crooked a finger at me. Excitement rushed through me as I took the few steps back to the exam table.

"Is my little slut trying to tease me?" This time he yanked me between his legs.

"What gave it away? My lack of panties?"

His cock began to press against the front of his gown. "Look what you've done."

I flipped what was left of my hair over my shoulder. "I don't care."

He breathed out hard through his nose. My sass was getting to him.

"I think you need a—"

There was a sharp knock at the door behind Braden. The nurse poked her head in. "Doctor Sullivan got caught up in the OR. He's running late. We expect him here in fifteen minutes or so."

"Thanks." I smiled as she shut the door.

"Fifteen minutes." I started to back away to grab my phone so I could text Kyrie that I wouldn't be back to work today.

Braden gripped my hips hard. "As I was saying before we were interrupted, I think you need a spanking."

Heat rushed over my skin like wildfire. "No. We can't do that in here." I glanced around at the sterile office, the white tile floors, and the very medical-looking cabinets and swabs.

"Maybe you should have thought of that before you decided to give me a view of that fine pussy when you know I can't sink my cock in you." He gave me the sexy smirk that always managed to make my knees go weak.

In a swift motion, he gripped my waist and flipped me over his knee. I squeaked in protest. "Braden, your knee—"

"Is in tip top shape for this little activity." He gripped the back of my neck and pushed so I laid flat against his thighs, my legs dangling in the air.

"The nurse could come in."

He rubbed my ass through the fabric of my skirt. "Then you should probably be quiet."

Smack. The sound was loud in my ears, but probably didn't go much farther than our room. The sting was bearable. At least it was, until he yanked my skirt up and gave me three more strikes on my bare skin in rapid succession. On the last one, I dug my nails into his calf and barely managed to stifle my cry.

He massaged the sting away, running his hand back and forth across my ass before delving lower.

I bucked, but his hand at my neck tightened. "Braden, we can't."

He slid his fingers through my slick folds and sank one inside me. "Shh."

I bit back my moan as he pumped in and out of me in a languid rhythm.

"That's my good little slut. Teasing me, getting me all worked up. Now you know what a bad idea that is."

I nodded, though being a tease skyrocketed up my list of "favorite things to do to Braden." He added a second finger and released my neck to run his hand along my back. When he leaned over to get a better view of what he was doing to my pussy, I thought I might combust. In and out, he slowly worked me into a frenzy.

When he drew his fingers to his mouth and licked them clean, I shuddered.

When the door opened and the doctor walked in, I screamed.

CHAPTER TWENTY

BRADEN

I LOOKED UP AS the familiar doctor walked through the door.

"Hey, Doc. Good to see you." My face had to be bright red as I lifted Nik from my lap. She stood up straight, covering her face with both hands. I wasn't sure how to play this one. It wasn't every day that my doctor caught me fingerblasting my girlfriend in his office. I decided to roll with it.

"Not sure if I'm familiar with that technique for examining a patient. What do you call that?" Doc chuckled and walked toward me.

"Oh my God." Nikki's words were muffled against one of her palms that she'd clapped over her mouth.

"So yeah, Doc, this is Nikki. Nikki, Doc."

Nikki held out a hand, still covering her eyes with the other. "It's, umm, nice to meet you."

Doc smiled and took Nikki's hand. My phone buzzed in my jeans across the room. Nikki hurried over, as if glad for the distraction, and dug it from my pocket. She handed it to me, and I swiped across the screen. It was Coach. "Just a sec, Doc."

Coach: What'd the doctor say?

I quickly typed back a reply.

Me: He just walked in. Patience, you old fucker. I'll let you know soon.

I started to hand the phone back to Nikki when it went off again.

Coach: Suck my dick. I want to know as soon as you do.

Me: You will. I promise, loverboy.

I laughed and gave the phone to Nikki, who stowed it in her bag. She returned to my side and grabbed my hand as the doctor faced me. He gave her a warm smile, and she squeezed my hand. They seemed to be over the initial embarrassment, at least. "It was just Coach." I shrugged.

"So why are you here?" He turned the warm smile on me.

A draft from the vent on the floor reminded me of the fact I was free balling, and a slight shudder rippled through me.

"Knee." I pointed at my leg. "The usual."

"Those do seem to be a problem with you catchers. How long has it been hurting?"

Nikki nudged me with a sharp elbow. I knew better than to lie. "A few weeks."

"Tell me what happened."

"I ripped a liner to left. All was fine the first few steps to first, and then—" I took in a long breath through my nose. "I felt a small pop, and pain radiated through my whole leg. It kind of went numb for a second."

"Hmm, I see." Doc reached down and lifted my gown enough to expose my knee.

"It's been getting worse. I can barely walk on it anymore."

"And you kept playing on it, didn't you? Despite the pain?" He shot me a hard glance.

"Yeah. It was stupid, I know."

"Well, you guys have a lot on the line with your bodies. You're not the only athlete to play hurt. Don't be too hard on yourself."

I grinned, and Nikki glared at Doc. He must have sensed her frustration, because his tone changed. "Don't get me wrong. It would've been better to come in right when it happened. I don't want you to make a habit of this."

"So what do you think is wrong?" Nikki folded her arms across her chest.

"Why don't you lie down, Braden, and let me feel around on it. If you don't mind."

Nikki snorted. "Sorry. Sorry."

I cracked a smile, loving every bit of her dirty mind. Pushing myself all the way up on the table, I laid on my back as Doc prodded my knee from every angle and watched my reactions. He gripped the ball of my foot, his other hand around my knee, and twisted my leg.

"Fucking, Christ!" I gripped the side of the exam table and winced.

"Okay. Sorry. I'm done." He released his hold on my leg.

"Is it bad?" Nikki cringed.

"Here's the thing, guys—knees are funny. There are a lot of things going on in there with every little movement. We need an MRI to know for sure." Doc glanced over at Nikki.

She didn't appear satisfied with his response. "Any *ballpark* guess?" She made air quotes with her fingers when she said "ballpark."

"It's probably your ACL. The pop you felt has me concerned that a ligament snapped or tore. *But* the fact it wasn't more pronounced gives me hope it might be less serious. I really don't feel comfortable guessing until I can see what's going on in there. It could've been that his knee just rolled out of place for a second, maybe stretched a few things out. He could've stepped on something in the base path and it's just bruised. So we just have to wait and see."

I sat up straight, but kept my eyes locked on the floor.

163

"I'm done. It's all going to be over."

Nik scooted closer to me and ran her fingers down the back of my arm. "That's not what he said. There's a chance. Right, Doc?"

"I need to order the MRI. I'll get you in right now. I know there's a radiologist on duty who can read it. We can get results in the next thirty minutes or so. Okay?"

I tilted my head up to Nik's face and then turned to Doc and nodded. "Okay. Let's do it."

"These things usually take weeks, and we're going to find out in thirty minutes. We're doing the best we can, so please just be patient a little while longer."

"Thanks, Doc."

The next thirty minutes was going to be the most torturous span of time in my life.

The end of my career was all I could think about as I sat on the cold metal in front of the big fucking machine. I had to take my mind off of it somehow as I laid down flat on my back. "Don't be getting all jealous now."

Nik stared back at me, puzzled. "What?"

I glanced to the MRI machine. "They're about to shove me all slow-like into this giant pussy magnet. I just want you to know that it's not by choice. I'm doing this because it's what you wanted." I gave a thumbs up to the giant metal box. "Been called a pussy magnet a time or two in my life too."

Nik snorted. "MRI pussy jokes, huh? You cheating bastard. How could you?"

"Just taking one for the team, baby. I'm doing this out of love."

The machine fired up and started to whir.

"Please hold still." It was the tech person's voice. "We're

just taking you in past the knee, that's it."

"Hear that, babe? Just the tip. Just for a second. Just to see how it feels." I stiffened my toes to the sound of Nik's giggling. We'd watched *Wedding Crashers* so Nik was now in on the jokes. "In and out all quick-like. Just a teaser."

The mechanical table moved me in and out a few times before the machine shut down. The tech walked around and helped me up before leading Nikki and I back to the same waiting room.

What was probably fifteen minutes seemed like hours as we waited for the doctor to return. Nikki was uncharacteristically silent as she sat next to me on the exam table. But she kept my hand in hers and leaned into me, giving support without saying a word. I'd told myself I wouldn't worry about anything until I knew what I was up against. It was silly to do otherwise.

Nikki and I jolted upright when we heard the door handle rattle. The doctor strolled in with a file full of pictures. Nikki's tiny hand squeezed around mine.

"It's good news, Braden."

Nikki and I both let out huge sighs. I turned and smiled at her.

"Well, not great news, but good. There's no visible ligaments that are detached or torn."

"Awesome!" Nikki squealed and clapped for a moment.

"Just, hang on a second, okay? I can see where your MCL is stretched though. It's most likely strained. That's what's causing you so much discomfort. There are a lot of nerves that run through that area of the knee. Playing hurt isn't helping it heal at all. It needs to tighten back up." He held up his hand and made a fist. "I don't know how you've managed the pain this long without resting. So I'm sorry to tell you this, but the season is over for you. It'll take several months to rehab it back to normal."

It was like a ton of bricks crushed me in the chest. My lungs deflated, and I dropped my face into my palms.

"Wait? You just said it wasn't torn. That everything was

good. You said that right?" Nikki turned to me. "I heard him say everything was fine. It was good news."

I could hear Nikki's scolding tone, but I couldn't bear the thought of looking at her. Tears started to well in my eyes, because I knew the one big truth with the people in the front office. It was all about perception. I was already a liability, and they would use any excuse they could to cut me loose. At best, they'd use it as leverage to pay me less on my next contract.

I finally lifted my head to the Doc and stared into his eyes. "So that's it? Has to be for the season?"

He placed a hand on my shoulder and squeezed. "I'm afraid so, son."

Nikki wrapped her arms around me. I caught her scowling at the doctor. It made me grin, knowing how much she wanted me to succeed and be healthy.

"It's okay, babe. He's just doing his job." My words had no effect, and Doc was kind enough to still be respectful.

"I'm sorry, Nikki. If I could fix him right now, I definitely would. I promise. I'll give you guys a minute. Braden, I'm going to write up a prescription to manage the pain, and you need to start rehab as soon as possible. I'll get you all the information and bring in a brace."

"Thanks again, Doc."

After the door closed, and Doc had left the room, Nikki sniffled. "We'll get a second opinion. He doesn't know shit."

I chuckled. "Babe, he's the leading knee specialist in the world." Somehow, I thought she might be more upset than I was. I'd expected worse news.

"Well—I just—there's someone better than him out there. And we'll find them today. I don't care."

I grabbed her by the arms and turned her to face me. Her eyes misted and her face tinged with a light pink. "It's okay. I'll deal. Somehow."

"Braden—" She placed her palms on my cheeks. "—you need to let it out. Don't do what you always do. This has to be torture for you."

166

I looked away and exhaled a long breath. "I know. You're right." I turned back to face her. "I'm fucking scared, babe. What if this is it? What if I never get to play ball again?" I nuzzled into her shoulder. It all hit me at once—anger, frustration, and sadness. I wanted to crawl into the corner and die, and at the same time I wanted to burn the building to the ground. I stared long and hard at her and the tears started to stream down my cheeks. "D-don't tell Easton."

"What? Why?" Nik's eyes widened at my words.

I wiped away the tears with my forearm. "He'll do something crazy. He might jeopardize his career. I can't let him do that. I'll tell him when the time is right. Just not now. Not until we know what's going to happen."

"Okay, babe. I'll do whatever you want. You know that." Nikki dragged her nails up and down my tricep.

"Can you bring me my phone? I need to text Coach."

"Sure." She hustled over and then returned with my phone.

I took it.

Me: Strained MCL. Out for season. A blowie would help ease the pain.

While I was chuckling, I caught Nikki leaning over my shoulder, reading my message.

"You two are ridiculous." She paced around the room.

All I could think about was leaving the team, leaving my city. I wouldn't even be able to fuck around with Coach anymore. I'd still be able to text him, but it wouldn't be the same. He was my mentor and a great friend. My phone vibrated in my hand.

Coach: I'm sorry. We'll figure it out. I need to meet with you as soon as you leave there. Can you come by the clubhouse?

Me: Sure

"I need to meet with Coach. Let's get out of here."

"Okay, babe." Nikki grabbed my arm like I was wheelchair bound to help me off the exam table.

I had all but my jeans on when Doc opened the door. "Hey, we need to put a brace on that knee. Give it some support."

"Good timing." I pushed myself up onto the examination table.

"I don't have to tell you how to use one of these." He made quick work of strapping everything into place.

"Nope. I'm indeed familiar."

"Thought so. I sent the paperwork over to the physical therapist's office. Let's do another appointment in two weeks to check your progress."

I stared at the floor, defeated. "Sounds good."

CHAPTER TWENTY-ONE
BRADEN

I WALKED THROUGH THE door to Coach's office and sat down in a chair in front of his desk. "So, about that blowie?" I made a show of starting to unzip my pants.

Coach shook his head and smiled. "You're such a little shit."

I sensed the goodbye speech was coming soon. Coach started to say something when his eyes grew big, and his face wrinkled. He stared at the door behind me. "What do you want?"

I whipped around, and Ingram was standing there with a smug grin on his face.

"Braden, we need a word with you upstairs." Ingram glared at Coach, but the corners of his lips turned up in the slightest hint of a smile. "Alone."

"The fuck he's going alone." Coach sprang up from his chair. "What's this about?"

"It's none of your concern, *Coach*." Ingram smirked. "It's a need-to-know meeting. And all you need to know is how to put together a winning team with the tools we provide you. This is outside of your domain."

Coach marched around me and was in Ingram's face in a heartbeat. "You're a little prick. You know that? Don't think you're going to walk in here and bully me and my players, asshole. I have a contract, and I have lawyers who know how to read the fucking thing. You're stuck with me for at least three more years. Now take your little spreadsheets and math, and get the fuck out of my office before I shove your head so far up your ass you enjoy yesterday's lunch for a second time."

"Threats of assault, weak one-liners." Ingram held his hand up and mocked Coach's rant by opening and closing his fingers against his thumb. "Get some new material, old man."

The asshole put his hand on my shoulder, and I wanted to crush his goddamn knuckles.

"Braden, we need a word. As soon as you and Coach are finished."

Coach started to talk and I held up my hand. "It's fine, Coach." I moved my gaze to Ingram. "I'll be up in a minute."

"Hurry it up." Ingram made sure to chuckle at Coach before he walked out of the room.

I stood outside the large, wooden door to Ingram's office before finally pushing it open. My heart dropped into my stomach when I saw the owners and higher-ups of the organization sitting around a conference table. They were all staring at me.

I glanced around the room at the ornate woodwork and fancy furniture. These assholes were so out of touch with the team. It was no wonder they made piss poor decisions constantly. But what did I know? I was an uneducated ballplayer, not a Harvard MBA.

Instinctively, I tried to hide my limp, but realized the show was over when I looked around. I hobbled to the open chair on my side of the table.

"Braden, have a seat." Ingram had a wide smile affixed to his smug face.

I couldn't burn any bridges in case there was still hope

they were going to keep me around. I'd be a fucking backup bullpen catcher for peanuts if it meant I could still come to the field every day.

I turned to the owner. "Art." I gave him a quick nod that he returned. "Jerry, Sam, Chris." I shook hands with a few who stood to greet me before I took my seat.

"We know about the knee." Ingram didn't waste any time getting to business.

"Yeah, I just got back from the—"

"It's irrelevant." Ingram cut me off and waved a hand in the air before I could finish my sentence.

I sensed tension in the room. I'd been a franchise player for seven seasons with the Ravens, ever since I'd been drafted. Many fans and commentators called me the face of the team. I knew most of these guys' families. I'd been to their houses for dinner and helped with their kids' little league teams. Ingram was the only one I didn't have a personal connection with.

"You haven't put up the numbers we need, all season. All of your stats are down. Now with the knee, you're even more of a liability. So we—"

A commotion rang out in the hallway. It was Ingram's secretary's voice. Her stern yells grew clearer with each second that passed. "They are in a meeting. I was told they were not to be disturbed. You can't just barge—"

"Get out of my way or I'll move you, Margaret!" Coach's voice. He burst through the door. His face was fiery red, and veins bulged from his neck. "This whole meeting in here is bull-fucking-shit, Ingram." Coach's head was on a swivel, eyeing every other face in the room. "And the rest of you goddamn know it. I've never been so ashamed to be a part of this organization. And I've been with you for fifteen fucking years."

"Coach, don't." I shook my head at him. I knew what he was doing. It wasn't worth it. It'd only mean both of us looking for a job instead of just me. We both knew what they were about to tell me. "It's not worth it. Just go cool off."

"See what I mean?" Ingram shrugged at the other guys in the room. "His own player gives better advice than he does." Ingram scoffed and turned his back to Coach.

"You little maggot-shitting cocksucker. I don't give a fuck if I lose my job. If he goes—" Coach shot a finger in my direction. "Then I go. See, that's your problem, you arrogant little prick. You want to quantify baseball and put everything in a pretty little number box. Baseball isn't an exact science. It's an art. That kid's leadership, attitude, and character are more valuable than any spreadsheet you can build. But you're such a pompous dick face that you can't see any of it through your massive ego."

"Coach. Please. Just go. I can handle this." He was going to lose his job, and it was all because of me.

"You shut it, Braden. This isn't about you. It's about his problem with *me*." He glared down the long table at Ingram. "He doesn't like the fact that I have a contract he can't touch. I'm a thorn in his side. And while he might not think that you and I are worth our money, the others in this room do. They know it. And it's keeping him from getting what he wants."

"You think you're irreplaceable? You're a dinosaur. Go on then. You can go with Braden wherever you want and be mediocre together for all I care." Ingram belted out a laugh. "You have no leverage here, *Coach*."

"I do."

Every head in the room whipped around to the giant that filled the entire door frame.

"This doesn't concern you, Holliday. This is a closed meeting." Ingram frowned.

Easton stalked toward Ingram. *Fuck.*

I shook my head. "E, you shouldn't be here, man."

Easton stopped next to me. I stared up at him, silently telling him to not make a scene while simultaneously swelling with gratitude that he'd even attempt it.

He paused for a brief moment, glancing down at me.

"No, *you* shouldn't be here."

I turned away, and caught Coach grinning his dick off at Ingram. He probably hoped Easton was about to pummel his face. Instead, Easton marched over and stood a few feet away from Ingram and folded his arms across his broad chest. He leaned down so that they were nose to nose and jabbed Ingram's chest with his index finger. "If he goes, I go."

Ingram chuckled. "You have a contract. Don't be stupid, Holliday. You just signed a new one before the season."

Easton glared back at him. "Do you think I'm more worried about breaking a contract than standing up for my best friend? You're an idiot if you believe that."

"Fine. You know what? Fuck it, Holliday. You can kick rocks too." Ingram started to pace, and Easton chuckled. Ingram turned to face him. "Well what's so damn funny?"

"This." Easton kept his gaze trained on Ingram, and hollered over his shoulder, "Fellas."

I watched the door, wondering what the hell Easton was up to. One by one, every player on the roster walked into the room. Ramirez was front and center, and shot me a wink. Each guy nodded to me and said, "Captain," before glaring at Ingram.

Ingram balled his hands into fists at his sides and started toward Coach. Easton stepped in his path and waggled a finger at him. Ingram's chest rose and fell in huge waves with each breath he took.

"I know Coach put all of you up to this. You old bastard. You think you're so smart. You're hurting the team with all of your bullshit."

The cogs started to turn in my head. Who put Easton and the guys up to this? It couldn't have been Coach. He didn't know in time to organize them all and get them together. Then it hit me all at once.

Nikki.

My heart swelled and a tingling sensation radiated up through my chest and face. She hadn't listened to me and went to Easton anyway. I'd been trying to protect him, but it was she who was protecting me. At that moment, something inside of me changed. I'd always believed I'd choose Nikki over baseball, but now I knew it in my heart. I couldn't explain it, but baseball became less important. I still loved it, but Nikki was front and center. She was more important than anything and anyone else in my life. If I didn't have her, I didn't have anything.

Ingram started another one of his rants and Art, the owner, rose to his feet. "I think I've seen enough here, Ingram."

Ingram whipped his head up to look at him with a puzzled stare. "What?"

"I think we need to reassess." He turned to me. "Braden, we know you need to rehab and can't play the rest of the season. The news hurts us as much as it hurts you. Trust me when I tell you that, son. We still want you in the dugout, leading in any capacity you're willing to take on."

Ingram laughed. "You have to be—"

Art glared in his direction and flexed his jaw, speaking through gritted teeth. "That's enough."

Ingram's face tightened into a mean glare. "You can't do this. You pay me to manage the business interests of this organization."

"Yes, and we have a board of directors to oversee your management of said affairs. We also have bylaws for situations like this. Or did you not do your due diligence before signing a *business* contract?"

"Well, umm, I—" Ingram hemmed and hawed.

"That's what I thought. We'll see how the rehab goes and offer Braden a one year contract at that time. We will reassess at the end of next season. Now, Ingram, you find a way to work together with this team—" He paused. "—who are the real reason we are all here in the first place, or you can find yourself at the end of a contract negotiation as well. Got me?"

Ingram stared at the ground and brushed his hands down

his slacks. "Understood."

"Good." Art turned back to me. "I hope you'll consider sticking with the Ravens, son. You've done so much for us. This is the least we can do to repay you for your years of service."

I walked to him as fast as I could without tweaking my knee, and shook his hand. Tears streamed down my face. "I won't let you down, sir."

"You never have, son. No reason to think you'd start now." Art strode toward the door.

Ingram followed with a look of defeat on his face. I hobbled over and took the brunt of a rowdy group hug from all the guys.

After a few moments, I grabbed Easton by the arm and stared up at his pretty-boy face. "Take me to her."

His keys jingled as he shook them in front of me. "I'm on it, *Captain.*"

CHAPTER TWENTY-TWO

NIKKI

THE SUN STREAMED THROUGH the small window in my new office, but I couldn't shake off the chill of worry. I forced myself to continue unpacking my things even though my thoughts constantly strayed to Braden and his meeting with the coach.

"Where do you want this?" Cyrus bustled in with a box of *Style and Substance* back issues.

I pointed to the empty spot on the floor next to my new love seat. "There."

He placed the box where I'd said and turned to me. Wearing a crisp button-down and well-fitting slacks, he was easily the handsomest man in the office, maybe the building. Having him under my thumb as an assistant should have cheered me. Instead, I was listless and distracted as I leaned against my desk.

He tilted his chin toward the vase of flowers on my desk. "Did you call your mom and thank her?"

I glanced at the tasteful arrangement of calla lilies she'd sent to congratulate me on my promotion. She'd written the card herself, telling me she was proud and entreating me to bring Braden by the house again—no games. On any other day, I would have done a cartwheel upon receiving such a message from her.

"Heard anything?" Cyrus perched next to me, his light cologne a perfect accent to his easy charm.

"Not since I spilled to Easton." I shouldn't have done it,

but I couldn't help it. Braden needed backup if he was going to have a chance at staying on with the Ravens. Easton was more than happy to lend a hand. In fact, I'd only gotten halfway through my spiel when I heard the distinct roar of his truck engine and squealing tires.

"I'm on my way, Nik. We'll keep him. I'll do whatever I have to do." The phone call had ended over an hour ago, but I'd had no word since.

Squeak … squeak.

"Oh, fuck." I couldn't deal with creepy Grady on top of everything else.

Cyrus snorted. The squeaking picked up its pace, and Grady shot by my office with a quickness I didn't know he possessed.

"What was that?"

"After you told me about your hair, I had a little chat with Grady in the mail room." Cyrus cracked his knuckles in an intimidating, slow way. "Suffice it to say, he won't be bothering you anymore. Kyrie, either. All your mail comes to me. So there's no reason for him to talk to you, much less get close enough to steal anything else from your person. If he even looks at you wrong, let me know."

"You did that for me?"

He smiled, and dimples appeared in his smooth cheeks. "Yep. I'm your bitch, after all. I'll do whatever I have to so that you and Kyrie stay happy."

"Thanks." I leaned over and bumped him with my elbow. "I appreciate it."

"Can I ask for one little thing in return, maybe?" He ran a hand through his naturally wavy hair.

"Sure."

"There's a girl in accounting, perfect hourglass, long dark hair. Do you know her name?"

"Clara."

"Thanks." He grinned. "Have I mentioned how happy I am the handbook didn't include a 'non-fraternization' policy?"

I laughed. "You didn't, but I approve of your tomcatting efforts. Get you some and tell me all about it afterwards. I need some spicy tales in my life."

"Will do." He stood and walked to my door. "I've got a few more boxes to get for you, and then I'll help you organize."

"Thanks."

"My pleasure." He strode into the hallway and out of sight.

"Did you see Grady move past here like he was at Daytona?" Kyrie walked in, her red dress saying 'sex kitten' and her prim black cardigan saying 'librarian'. So, I supposed the mix said 'sex librarian.'

"Yeah, apparently Cyrus had a chat with him after the hair incident."

Kyrie laughed. "Easton actually asked me if I'd done something to my hair. All this time, he'd never noticed when I got a haircut, but after just one trip to Salon de Pervert, he was all over it."

I smiled, but couldn't quite make it to a laugh.

She sighed and opened her arms. "Come here."

I went to her. My eyes began to sting, and I fought back my tears. "What if they release him? What if he gets traded?"

"Shh." She ran her hand through my hair. "You're on the jump-to-conclusions mat. Step away from it and relax. There's no point worrying until we hear from him, okay?"

I nodded and moved my head down to snuggle into her chest. Her big, fluffy tits had always been soothing.

"Easton hasn't texted either?"

"No. You know I'd tell you first thing." She held me for a while, waiting for me to sack up and step away. It was hard to do when her tits were made to be the perfect comfort pillows.

"Everything will work out, you know?" She gave me a hard squeeze.

"I know." I straightened and wiped a tear from each side of my face. "I'm okay." Looking around at my boxed-up office, I sighed. "I need to unpack anyway. Should take my mind off it."

Kyrie walked over to the love seat and ran her hand across the brown leather. "This looks perfect in here. You won't be able to get me out of your office."

I smiled. "Good. I have no clue what I'm doing so your help is kind of important."

She pointed at a bare spot in the back corner near the window. "Get a mini-fridge with some booze in it, and I'll talk to Graciela about taking the wall down between our offices."

"Will do." I managed a small chuckle before locking my gaze with hers. "And thank you. For everything."

She waved a nonchalant hand. "Don't worry about it. I'm always here for you. No matter what."

"So am I." Braden's voice sounded in the hallway and he appeared in my doorway, a huge grin on his face.

I darted to him, and he caught me in his arms. "What's the news. Is it okay? Are you—"

He bent me back and claimed my mouth in a kiss that made my knees turn to jelly. His tongue teased my lips, then sank into my mouth as my eyes fluttered closed.

"I'll just be outside." Kyrie edged past us and into the hallway.

Braden ran one hand down to my ass and squeezed, his deep groan vibrating from his chest to mine. He lifted me and carried me into my office despite his limp. With a kick and a groan, he shut my door. Pulling me up so I had no choice but to wrap my legs around him, he kissed down my neck.

Heat flashed across my skin, and my pussy went from desert to rainforest in moments.

"So, good news?" I squirmed as his cock hardened against me and his lips traveled lower.

"I'm staying on. Now stop talking and let me fuck you in your new office like the little slut you are."

I moaned right as loud music started playing in Kyrie's

office next door. That little bitch was covering for me, and I loved her for it.

Worry had me struggling to get free of his grip, but it was no use. "Braden, you'll get me fired."

He laid me down on my loveseat and crushed me with his weight. "I guess that means you need to be quiet." One palm slapped over my mouth, and he used the other to hike my skirt up.

When he grazed my wet panties, he thrust his hips against me. "I'm going to push these to the side and sink my cock inside you until you come. Then I'm going to give you every last drop."

My thighs went up in flames as he lifted up to unbutton his jeans and pull them down. His thick cock sprang free from his boxers. I whimpered when he settled on top of me again and his fingers pushed my panties all the way to the side as promised.

"Is *this* what you want, my little slut?" He surged forward with his hips, rubbing his smooth cock against my clit as he pinned me with his body.

I nodded, and he covered my mouth again. Lifting my hips, I moaned when he plunged inside me. My eyes rolled back in my head as he started a hard rhythm, grinding against me as he bit and sucked my neck. I inched my leg higher until I hooked my heel against the top of the loveseat. Each hard thrust hit my clit, and I angled myself so that he went deep enough to hit my spot.

"That's it. I know how my perfect slut likes it." He bit my ear, filth falling from his lips and sending me higher. "I love this wet little cunt. I'm going to leave it messy. Then when you get home, I'm going to fuck it again, because it's mine."

I moaned loud, but he caught it with his palm and gave me a devilish smirk. "Tell me it's mine. I want to hear it." He released his grip on my mouth.

I gasped as he surged inside me, keeping his strokes hard and deep. He groaned when I ran my nails down his back.

"Say it. Who owns this pussy?"

"You do." It was more of a whine than anything else. The thrill of being caught was like gasoline on the fire, and I was already losing myself in pleasure.

"That's right. Whose slut are you?"

All my tension pooled in my clit, and each thrust from Braden sent me closer to the edge. I gasped when he bit my neck. "Yours, only yours."

"That's right." He slapped his palm back over my mouth and shoved forward even harder until the vase on my desk rattled with his impacts.

My hips began to seize, and Braden bore down, grinding his hips on my clit. I came with a moan, my eyes clenching shut as he worked my body.

"Fucking hell." His hips thrust forward and his cock kicked inside me as he grunted and slowed his pace.

Starbursts lit the back of my eyelids, and I was faintly aware of the music next door quieting down. I gulped in air when Braden removed his hand, but he quickly replaced it with his lips. He kissed me gently, his tongue giving loving strokes. I hugged him close as happiness welled inside me.

He pulled away and stared into my eyes. "That was hot as fuck."

I smiled and leaned up to give him another kiss. "Agreed."

He sat back and pulled his boxers and jeans back in place. Then he arranged my panties for me and smoothed down my skirt.

"I need to go to the bathr—"

"I don't think so." He bent down and kissed me hard. "I want you wearing me for the rest of the day."

My pussy quivered at his filthy request. He smirked.

A thump sounded from next door and the music grew louder again. I could hear a soft moan nearby, as if Kyrie were against the wall that separated our offices.

I cocked my head to the side. "Easton?"

He sat back and pulled me up to sit next to him. "Fucking stealing my thunder over there. Acting like it was his idea to fuck his woman at the office. Come here." He lifted me so I sat in his lap sideways.

My heart still thundered as I tried to come down from the high he'd given me. "So you're staying?"

He ran his hand down my back. "*We're* staying. Easton pulled some 'oh captain, my captain' shit without the homosexual undertones. It worked. Management is keeping me around while I heal up, and I'll play next season if all goes well."

I cradled his face in my hands. "I'm so happy I might just shit a rainbow."

He laughed as another thump and a squeal carried from next door.

"I'm happy, too. But—" He pulled me into his chest. "—I want you to know that while baseball makes me happy, nothing beats the way I feel when I'm with you. *You're* my life, Nikki. Not the game. Not my career. *You.*"

I pulled back and stared into his earnest eyes. "Do you mean it?"

"I've never been more serious about anything in my life." His voice trembled and his eyes began to sparkle with tears. "Nobody has ever done anything like that for me before. I love you."

"I'd do it again. I love you too, baby." I wrapped my arms around his neck and smiled. "It looks like I chased the right set of cleats."

He hovered his lips over mine, promising me another breathtaking kiss. "And I've made the perfect catch."

EPILOGUE

NIKKI

6 months later

THE STADIUM ROARED ON all sides, creating a wall of sound to greet the Ravens as they took the field on Opening Day. I rose to my feet and screamed for Braden as he trotted from the dugout and gave me a wide smile.

"Is it always this hot?" My mother clicked open an ornate pink fan.

"It's springtime. Perfect baseball weather."

The Opening Day magic floated in the air, brightening the grass, giving the sky a little extra blue, and making a World Series season seem possible. The baseball gods smiled as the players got ready to begin the inning.

I brought my gaze back down to the player who stole my heart. Braden kicked up some dirt at home plate as the first batter for the Sentinels took some practice swings.

"Hey, catcher! Go easy on those knees." Kasey cupped her hands around her mouth. "You'll have to use them later when you take a big ol' Easton-dog right in your kisser!"

I turned and gave her a pointed glare, then glanced to my family and back to her.

She shrugged. "What?"

Mom covered her face with her fan and shook her head.

"Oh, come on, Cat. It's all in good fun." Dad wrapped his arm around her shoulders.

She peeked over her fan as Braden waved at me and then

185

gave Kasey the finger.

I laughed, joy bubbling inside me at how natural he looked on the field. His rehab had gone well, and his MCL had healed without any lingering pain or problems. Today was the test, though—the first full game since he was pulled last season. I'd done some extra bedazzling on my tank top and shorty shorts with his number, and I'd forced Kyrie into wearing my bedazzled gifts, too. We were the team's number one fans, and we bore bedazzled proof.

"Ball parks never change. It smells the same way it did when I was twelve years old." Ben looped his arm across the back of Kasey's chair. "What do you think, Kase? Are the Ravens going to bring this game home?"

"Not with shitnuts as catcher and cuntflaps as pitcher, no." She grinned, tossed a piece of popcorn in the air, and caught it in her mouth.

"Come on. Why so little faith?" Ben had a crush on Kasey since they first met over Christmas break. He couldn't come to terms with the fact that she wasn't into men. It was kind of cute, if doomed.

"Have you ever heard of a little something called a jinx?" Kasey slapped him on the side of his head. "I'm not going to say what I really think lest the baseball gods come down on us. So just agree with me that we're fucked."

"Totally fucked." He nodded.

The umpire yelled to get the game going, and the crowd roared with approval. My stomach twisted in a knot as Braden hunkered down behind the plate and Parham took the mound.

"How long do you think it will take for them to score a goal?" My mom stowed her fan and pulled out her phone.

"Mom, pay attention. This is important to me." I took my seat next to her. "And to Braden."

Braden had managed to smooth over the ruffled feathers from his first meeting with my parents. We'd spent the Christmas break in Florida at my parents' house. He'd charmed them with his baseball tales to the point that even

Mom warmed to him. It didn't hurt that she'd discovered the number of zeroes attached to the end of his salary as starting catcher for the Ravens. I hadn't heard so much as a peep from her about Carter since the incident outside the restaurant.

"And please don't ever say 'score a goal' in the ballpark ever again." My dad's eyes were bright and focused on the game.

"Or whatever it is they do." She waved her hand at the batter who swung and missed on his first pitch.

Braden threw the ball back to Parham and squatted back behind the plate. Two more strikes, and the hitter was out.

It was an almost even game for the first few innings. But in the sixth, when Braden knocked in two runs with a shot down the first base line, the Ravens went up by four. The stadium relaxed, though opening day excitement still maintained a hum of adrenaline.

"I'm going to get some more beer." Kasey stood during the seventh inning stretch. "Anyone want?"

Ben scrambled to his feet. "I'll go with you."

Kasey put a hand to his chest. "No thanks. Your trouser snake will scare away all the pussy. I can't have you cramping my game."

Mom slapped Kasey's leg. "Honestly. Do you *really* have to be so vulgar all the time?"

Kasey smirked. "Yeah, pretty much. So, you feeling a Bud, Mrs. Graves?"

Mom sighed. "I'll have a Stella in a nice glass. If they don't have a nice glass, make sure whatever they put it in is clean."

"Yes, ma'am. I'll spit shine it myself if I have to." Kasey took the stadium steps two at a time, and Ben sank down next to me.

I patted his knee. "It's never going to happen. You know this, right?"

"I don't know what you're talking about." He trained his eyes on Parham, whose arm was starting to fade.

187

"Kasey is a poon-hound. Trust me. Remember when she groped my tits on national TV?"

"Yeah." He snorted. "That was pretty funny."

"That's who she is. You aren't going to change her. Trust me."

"I guess you're right. She's just so …"

"Not for you." I kept my tone emphatic.

"I got it loud and clear. I have plenty of other prospects." He shrugged. "Kasey isn't the only poon-hound around here."

I pretended to vomit. "Yick."

Kyrie jumped up and darted to the net. "Easton's coming out!"

"I knew he liked the cock all along." Kasey had returned and handed a beer to my mother.

She took a big swig of her own and smacked Kyrie on the ass as she walked past.

Kyrie shot her a glare. "You know what I mean."

Braden stood and ran out to the mound to greet him. But halfway there, he took an odd step. My breath caught in my throat. I watched in horror as he collapsed, his knee giving way. Mom clutched my hand.

"Shit." Kasey drew out the word as Easton ran to Braden.

Easton hit the turf and felt around on Braden's knee as his teammates began to draw in closer. I couldn't blink, my eyes riveted on Braden as he gripped his knee and rolled back and forth. The Coach came from the dugout and called time while he went to investigate. *Please no, please no, please God no.*

The Coach bent over and had a word before backing away and talking to the ump. Easton got to his feet, then helped Braden onto his good leg. He hobbled a few steps, until Easton scooped him up and threw him over his shoulder.

Instead of walking to the dugout, Easton carried him to the wall at the edge of the net. I dashed over and pushed through the fans with Kyrie right behind me. My eyes watered as Easton set Braden down on his good leg.

Leaning over the brick wall, I saw the tears in his eyes. Then he fell, dropping to his knee. Easton followed him down, both of them sobbing, their faces turned toward the grass.

"Oh my God, is it that bad?" I put a hand to my mouth.

"It's really bad, Nik." Braden's voice shook.

I clenched my eyes shut as dread washed through me. Had the MCL finally pulled all the way free?

"A game changer." Easton slapped Braden on the back.

"A show stopper. All over, man. For the both of us."

They reached into their pockets.

My brain couldn't process it. Why were they on their knees and holding velvet ring boxes? The crowd around me began to titter and yell, and then the entire stadium started cheering as my shocked face was broadcast on the giant monitors. Kyrie gripped my elbow as we both stared down at the tricksters in the grass holding diamond rings.

"Fuckbags been running a game on us." Kasey leaned on the brick wall to get a better view of Braden and Easton and the rings they offered. "Nice hardware, though. Someone with *excellent* taste must have helped pick them out." She gave a self-satisfied smirk.

I swallowed hard, and Kyrie began to tremble at my side.

Easton grinned. "Kyrie—"

Braden grinned even bigger. "Nikki—"

In unison they asked, "Will you marry me?"

Dark Romance by Celia Aaron

SINCLAIR
The Acquisition Series, Prologue

Sinclair Vinemont, an impeccable parish prosecutor, conducts his duties the same way he conducts his life-- every move calculated, every outcome assured. When he sees something he wants, he takes it. When he finds a hint of weakness, he capitalizes. But what happens when he sees Stella Rousseau for the very first time?

COUNSELLOR
The Acquisition Series, Book 1

In the heart of Louisiana, the most powerful people in the South live behind elegant gates, mossy trees, and pleasant masks. Once every ten years, the pretense falls away and a tournament is held to determine who will rule them. The Acquisition is a crucible for the Southern nobility, a love letter written to a time when barbarism was enshrined as law.

Now, Sinclair Vinemont is in the running to claim the prize. There is only one way to win, and he has the key to do it—Stella Rousseau, his Acquisition. To save her father, Stella has agreed to become Sinclair's slave for one year. Though she is at the mercy of the cold, treacherous Vinemont, Stella will not go willingly into darkness.

As Sinclair and Stella battle against each other and the clock, only one thing is certain: The Acquisition always ends in blood.

MAGNATE
The Acquisition Series, Book 2

Lucius Vinemont has spirited me away to a world of sugar cane and sun. There is nothing he cannot give me on his lavish Cuban plantation. Each gift seduces me, each touch seals my fate. There is no more talk of depraved competitions or his older brother – the one who'd stolen me, claimed me, and made me feel things I never should have. Even as Lucius works to make me forget Sinclair, my thoughts stray back to him, to the dark blue eyes that haunt my sweetest dreams and bitterest nightmares. Just like every dream, this one must end. Christmas will soon be here, and with it, the second trial of the Acquisition.

SOVEREIGN
The Acquisition Series, Book 3

The Acquisition has ruled my life, ruled my every waking moment since Sinclair Vinemont first showed up at my house offering an infernal bargain to save my father's life. Now I know the stakes. The charade is at an end, and Sinclair has far more to lose than I ever did. But this knowledge hasn't strengthened me. Instead, each revelation breaks me down until nothing is left but my fight and my rage. As I struggle to survive, only one question remains. How far will I go to save those I love and burn the Acquisition to the ground?

Sports Romance by Celia Aaron

KICKED

Trent Carrington.

Trent Mr. Perfect-Has-Everyone-Fooled Carrington.

He's the star quarterback, university scholar, and happens to be the sexiest man I've ever seen. He shines at any angle, and especially under the Saturday night stadium lights where I watch him from the sidelines. But I know the real him, the one who broke my heart and pretended I didn't exist for the past two years.

I'm the third-string kicker, the only woman on the team and nothing better than a mascot. Until I'm not. Until I get my chance to earn a full scholarship and join the team as first-string. The only way I'll make the cut is to accept help from the one man I swore to never trust again. The problem is, with each stolen glance and lingering touch, I begin to realizing that trusting Trent isn't the problem. It's that I can't trust myself when I'm around him.

Short, Sexy Reads by Celia Aaron

A Stepbrother for Christmas
The Hard and Dirty Holidays

Annalise dreads seeing her stepbrother at her family's Christmas get-together. Niles had always been so nasty, tormenting her in high school after their parents had gotten married. British and snobby, Niles did everything he could to hurt Annalise when they were younger. Now, Annalise hasn't seen Niles in three years; he's been away at school in England and Annalise has started her pre-med program in Dallas. When they reconnect, dark memories threaten, sparks fly, and they give true meaning to the "hard and dirty holidays."

Bad Boy Valentine
The Hard and Dirty Holidays

Jess has always been shy. Keeping her head down and staying out of sight have served her well, especially when a sexy photographer moves in across the hall from her. Michael has a budding career, a dark past, and enough ink and piercings to make Jess' mouth water. She is well equipped to watched him through her peephole and stalk him on social media. But what happens when the bad boy next door comes knocking?

F*ck of the Irish
The Hard and Dirty Holidays

Eamon is my crush, the one guy I can't stop thinking about. His Irish accent, toned body, and sparkling eyes captivated me the second I saw him. But since he slept with my roommate, who claims she still loves him, he's been off limits. Despite my prohibition on dating him, he has other other ideas. Resisting him is the key to keeping my roommate happy, but giving in may bring me more pleasure than I ever imagined.

Forced by the Kingpin
Forced Series, Book 1

I've been on the trail of the local mob kingpin for months. I know his haunts, habits, and vices. The only thing I didn't know was how obsessed he was with me. Now, caught in his trap, I'm about to find out how far he and his local cop-on-the-take will go to keep me silent.

Forced by the Professor
Forced Series, Book 2

I've been in Professor Stevens' class for a semester. He's brilliant, severe, and hot as hell. I haven't been particularly attentive, prepared, or timely, but he hasn't said anything to me about it. I figure he must not mind and intends to let me slide. At least I thought that was the case until he told me to stay after class today. Maybe he'll let me off with a warning?

Forced by the Hitmen
Forced Series, Book 3

I stayed out of my father's business. His dirty money never mattered to me, so long as my trust fund was full of it. But now I've been kidnapped by his enemies and stuffed in a bag. The rough men who took me have promised to hurt me if I make a sound or try to run. I know, deep down, they are going to hurt me no matter what I do. Now I'm cuffed to their bed. Will I ever see the light of day again?

Forced by the Stepbrother
Forced Series, Book 4

Dancing for strange men was the biggest turn on I'd ever known. Until I met him. He was able to control me, make me hot, make me need him, with nothing more than a look. But he was a fantasy. Just another client who worked me up and paid my bills. Until he found me, the real me. Now, he's backed me into a corner. His threats and promises, darkly whispered in tones of sex and violence, have bound me surer than the cruelest ropes. At first I was unsure, but now I know – him being my stepbrother is the least of my worries.

Forced by the Quarterback
Forced Series, Book 5

For three years, I'd lusted after Jericho, my brother's best friend and quarterback of our college football team. He's never paid me any attention, considering me nothing more than a little sister he never had. Now, I'm starting freshman year and I'm sharing a suite with my brother. Jericho is over all the time, but he'll never see me as anything other than the shy girl he met three years ago. But that's not who I am. Not really. To get over Jericho – and to finally get off – I've arranged a meeting with HardcoreDom. If I can't have Jericho, I'll give myself to a man who will master me, force me, and dominate me the way I desperately need.

***

Zeus
Taken by Olympus, Book 1

One minute I'm looking after an injured gelding, the next I'm tied to a luxurious bed. I never believed in fairy tales, never gave a second thought to myths. Now that I've been kidnapped by a man with golden eyes and a body that makes my mouth water, I'm not sure what I believe anymore. . . But I know what I want.

***

Cash Remington
and the Missing Heiress
Sexy Dreadfuls, Book 1

I'm the best operator in the entire agency. The plum assignments—always mine. So when an American heiress goes missing, I'm the guy they call to get her back. Rescuing Collette Stanford is my mission. What I do to her after that is purely up to me, as long as she makes it back to the States in one piece. I'll kill the bad guys, get the girl, and get a little taste of what the heiress has to offer. None of this is negotiable. I'm Cash Remington, and I never miss.

Cash Remington
and the Rum Run
Sexy Dreadfuls, Book 2

I plunder the sea, steal what I can, and never look back. It's a pirate captain's life for me. When my crew and I discover a destroyed ship floating on the endless waves, we scavenge it for every scrap of cloth and every morsel of food. Inside, I find a treasure—gold, gems, and a girl. I'll ravage the girl, spend the gold, and use the gem to buy the ship of my dreams—the Gloomy Lotus. At least that's the plan—until the Kraken, a whirlpool, and a six-headed beast attack my ship. Despite the danger, I still intend to have my way with the girl. Nothing can stop me. I'm Cash Remington, and I take what I want.

Novels by Sloane Howell

The Matriarch:
An Erotic Superhero Romance
The Matriarch Trilogy, Book 1

Betrayal is easy, sex is a weapon, and information is power. Maggie Madison sits in the lofty towers of her city during the day, but at night she lurks the seedy underbelly, looking to snare the man who stole her innocence. Her simple quest becomes complicated when she meets a man who is as light as she is dark, as straightforward as she is deceptive. When a villain rises and sets her world alight, she must weigh her need for revenge against the good of the city she vowed to protect.

PANTY WHISPERER
The Complete Series

I love women. I'm not ashamed to admit that making a beautiful woman come is my main goal in life—one that I accomplish night after night. Women are as drawn to me as I am to them. I don't get turned down. It's not a brag, just a fact. At least it was a fact. Until I met Quinn—the one woman who didn't fall for my easy charm. Now, I have to have her. She may not want to get close, may not want to admit that I turn her on and can give her a night that she'll never forget, but she was mine the first moment I saw her. Eventually, I'll have her beneath me, my hands in her hair, and my name on her lips. It's what I do. I'm the Panty Whisperer.

Shorts and Novellas by Sloane Howell

The Panty Whisperer: Volume 1
The Panty Whisperer Series, Book 1

Have you ever been pushed to the edge, and then over it? Have you ever had your toes cramp and your head shoot to the sky, trying to log every touch, every feeling in your memory, to reenact every situation later in the shower, or underneath your cool bed sheets? Have you ever had someone own your mind, penetrating every single one of your sexual fantasies, unable to shake free of them?

The thought of me will be a thirst you can' t quench, an itch you just can' t scratch, a drug that you cannot have. Every time you run your fingers down over your body, longing for that unattainable feeling I gave you, that warm sensation shooting into your toes, that complete surrender of all inhibition, aching for me to have you just one more time, I' ll be there, inside your mind...

My name is Joel Hannover and I am the panty whisperer. Some men are good at business, some gifted at mathematics--I' m good at making women come, hard. It' s a gift I' ve possessed my entire life. If there was a girl nobody could bed, I was the first to get there. I always get there. I work as an accounting software consultant. That' s a fancy way of saying I' m a salesman. Accounting departments are full of women, dressed conservatively, presumed to live boring, mundane lives. Nothing could be further from the truth. These women are unique, sexual creatures, yearning for someone to take them to their breaking point and beyond.

Jessica Moore is one such woman, mid-thirties, bad marriage, basically raising the kids all on her own. She is sexy as hell, she just doesn't know what she's capable of. Will I give her everything she longs for? You'll just have to read to find out...

The Panty Whisperer, Volumes 1 - 5
The Panty Whisperer Series, Books 1 - 5

This collection includes the original plus four additional fast-paced, panty-dropping short stories.

Have you ever been pushed to the edge, and then over it? Have you ever had your toes cramp and your head shoot to the sky, trying to log every touch, every feeling in your memory, to reenact every situation later in the shower, or underneath your cool bed sheets? Have you ever had someone own your mind, penetrating every single one of your sexual fantasies, unable to shake free of them?

The thought of me will be a thirst you can't quench, an itch you just can't scratch, a drug that you cannot have. Every time you run your fingers down over your body, longing for that unattainable feeling I gave you, that warm sensation shooting into your toes, that complete surrender of all inhibition, aching for me to have you just one more time, I'll be there, inside your mind...

My name is Joel Hannover and I am the panty

whisperer. Some men are good at business, some gifted at mathematics--I'm good at making women come, hard. It's a gift I've possessed my entire life. If there was a girl nobody could bed, I was the first to get there. I always get there. I work as an accounting software consultant. That's a fancy way of saying I'm a salesman. Accounting departments are full of women, dressed conservatively, presumed to live boring, mundane lives. Nothing could be further from the truth. These women are unique, sexual creatures, yearning for someone to take them to their breaking point and beyond.

Will Joel finally meet his match? You'll have to read to find out...

The Panty Whisperer, Volume 6
The Panty Whisperer Series, Book 6

Has Joel finally met his match?

This is a follow up novella to the first five short stories in The Panty Whisperer serial.

Have you ever been pushed to the edge, and then over it? Have you ever had your toes cramp and your head shoot to the sky, trying to log every touch, every feeling in your memory, to reenact every situation later in the shower, or underneath your cool bed sheets? Have you ever had someone own your mind, penetrating every single one of your sexual fantasies, unable to shake free of them?

The thought of me will be a thirst you can't quench, an itch you just can't scratch, a drug that you cannot have.

Every time you run your fingers down over your body, longing for that unattainable feeling I gave you, that warm sensation shooting into your toes, that complete surrender of all inhibition, aching for me to have you just one more time, I'll be there, inside your mind...

My name is Joel Hannover and I am the panty whisperer. Some men are good at business, some gifted at mathematics--I'm good at making women come, hard. It's a gift I've possessed my entire life. If there was a girl nobody could bed, I was the first to get there. I always get there. I work as an accounting software consultant. That's a fancy way of saying I'm a salesman. Accounting departments are full of women, dressed conservatively, presumed to live boring, mundane lives. Nothing could be further from the truth. These women are unique, sexual creatures, yearning for someone to take them to their breaking point and beyond.

How will Joel cope with Quinn's rejection? You'll have to read to find out...

***

Chloe Comes For Christmas, An Erotic Holiday Novella

James lives in the friend zone. His best friend and fraternity brother Mark, the All-American cornerback, has always found a way to get the girl going back to their teens. When James meets Chloe first and falls for her, Mark swoops in once again.

This time is different though. James has his sights on teaching them both a lesson for making him look the fool.

***

Bad Boy Revelation
The Alpha Bad Boy Series, Book 1

Daddy told me not to even look at the man in the corner. He's troubled he said. I wanted to do more than look at him.

I grew up in the church. I was raised better. And I was broken. Oh, was I ever broken. I had a sexual appetite that couldn't be filled. A thirst in me that only sin could quench. I needed him, the man in the corner, to claim me, dominate me, own me.

I'd do whatever it took. Goad him if necessary. I needed that man like I needed air or water. I needed the bad boy.

Bad Boy Prospect
The Alpha Bad Boy Series, Book 2

Fighting, f***ing, and winning. It's what I do and nobody will stand in my way. It's how I live my life on the field and in the bedroom. I make hitters fear me. If they're scared, it gives me an advantage, and I capitalize on it. People say I have an attitude problem, that I'm a bad boy. It's exactly what I want them to think.

Until I meet Elizabeth, the psychiatrist Coach makes me see. She specializes in pro athletes. There's something about her. Maybe she'll be the one who finally cuts through my layers and sees the real me. Who knows?

Bad Boy Brawler
The Alpha Bad Boy Series, Book 3

Devyn O'Dare is the Ultra MMA world heavyweight champion. He destroys opponents. He doesn't like to be in the public eye. One day he makes a bad decision that will alter his life forever.

In the hospital he meets Carly, single mom, nurse, struggling day to day. Devyn feels he can right some wrongs from his troubled past. He can change Carly's life and end her struggles, prevent her son from the same type of childhood he experienced. But Carly must decide if she wants to trust Devyn and put her pride aside, or soldier through life alone with her son.

Bad Boy Con Man
The Alpha Bad Boy Series, Book 4

Grayson is a con man. If he sees an opportunity, he capitalizes. When the score that can set him up for life comes along it's too much for him to resist.

Then he meets Amelia. Intelligent, funny, gorgeous, and a lover of comic books. She's everything he's ever wanted. But, at the end of the day he has to make a choice — hurt the woman he's crazy about, or take the money and leave his old life behind.

***

Payne Capital
The Payne Capital Series, Book 1

Devyn White and his fiancee Meredith—the perfect All-American couple—have just moved to New York City following his acceptance of his dream job working at Payne Capital, a private equity firm ran by Rebekah Payne, a billionaire math and finance prodigy. Devyn soon realizes his dream isn' t all that he imagined as he is thrust into ethical dilemmas involving an ex-husband, an out of control boss, the operations of the firm, and his own personal relationship with Meredith. When the heat is turned up he must soon make difficult choices that will affect the rest of his life and possibly hurt the people he loves in the process.

Printed in Great Britain
by Amazon